THE GOLDEN PHOENIX

A Supernatural Crime Romance Thriller

KAREN POWER

Published by Karen Power

Copyright ©2021. The moral right of Karen Power to be identified as the Author of the work has been asserted by her in accordance with the Copyright, Designs and Patents Act 1988. All rights reserved. No part of this book may be used or reproduced by any means, graphic, electronic, or mechanical, including photocopying, recording, taping or by any information storage retrieval system without the written permission of the publisher except in the case of brief quotations embodied in critical articles and reviews.

This novel is entirely a work of fiction. The names, characters and incidents portrayed are the work of the author's imagination. Any resemblances to actual persons, living or dead, events or localities are entirely coincidental.

ISBN: 978-1-7635753-0-1 (paperback)
ISBN 978-1-7635753-1-8 (e-book)
ISBN: 978-0-6450435-7-0 (audiobook)

Book cover art concept: Karen Power

 A catalogue record for this book is available from the National Library of Australia

DEDICATION

To my Mum, my friends, and all the people who have helped me along my creative journey in this lifetime. I thank you with love.

Karen Power xoxo

One

The Year Set 1997.

Kirsten swiftly runs toward Linda, calling out, "Quick Linda, it's an 801 on the Police radio, it's Shane, he's on High Street at the Driveway Chicken Shop in Reservoir." Linda and Kirsten quickly jump into the Police Car. Linda starts up the engine, switching the Police Patrol Car siren on full bore. They swiftly speed off down the road at 100 miles an hour. The Police Patrol Car tears through the takeaway shop driveway. Suddenly, the Police Patrol Car comes to a screeching halt. The Police siren shuts down automatically as a young girl about sixteen runs out from the takeaway shop, narrowly missing getting run over by the Police Patrol Car. In shock, the teenage girl stops dead in her tracks. Terrified, she drops the red and white striped boxes she holds in her hands, and an ear-piercing eerie scream hysterically erupts from her fearful heart. "We've been robbed. The robbers went that way", rigorously waving Kirsten and Linda in the direction the two young offenders had fled, yelling repeatedly, "The robbers went that way." Swiftly in the same direction, the Police Patrol Car rapidly shoots off down the road quickly to back up their co-worker Shane. Linda relished the fast-driving side of the job when it arose and had no hesitation running the full gauntlet of the adrenaline rush in any given situation. Linda was heavily into car racing and loved every minute of it. She spent hours at the race track pursuing her passion. It appealed to the wild side of her ballsy nature. Kirsten, now tense, sat in the passenger seat, twisting her long, loose red curl that had escaped her ponytail. Kirsten was a much slower driver. Due to the unfortunate experience over a couple of years of pulling dead decapitated bodies out from smashed-up vehicles. Kirsten had a prior nursing background working in rehabilitation, tending brutally injured victims of road accidents with chronically mangled and dysfunctional limbs back into some working order. She sat rigid and calm when inside. The sound of her loud heartbeat pulsating was deafening to her ears, but who was to know? Focusing on the job at hand, Kirsten hoped that her precious Shane was O.K. and didn't injure himself in any way, especially now as he was so close to reaching his goal to participate in an upcoming bodybuilding competition. Shane's strong, manly voice came over the Police Patrol Car Radio, indicating that he had lost sight of the two young robbers. His updated report was that the two Offenders running on foot had disappeared. Shane instructed Kirsten and Linda that he was lapping the block. The staffing shortage today has made the job difficult due to recent Government cutbacks. There were only three of them involved in this high-speed car pursuit. Kirsten and Linda decided to head off in the opposite direction, opting to shoot down a backstreet. Kirsten spots two figures running frantically down the road up ahead, observing them madly jumping fences and dangerously hurdling large container rubbish bins, momentarily disappearing as they dart across a large deserted concrete Industrial area. Linda following promptly sped up in hot pursuit of the Offenders. The Police Patrol Car slows as Linda and Kirsten approach a petrol garage. Thinking perhaps the two offenders had got away, Linda impulsively hits the brakes, instinctively deciding to turn the Police Patrol Car around and return for a second search. Then, they observe a small green car swerving recklessly out of the service station. The two young offenders had now hijacked a car. Its owner had left the car running with keys in the ignition while he'd run in to pay for his petrol. On went the Police siren again, high octave, loud and extremely ear-piercing. The small green car the Police were in pursuit of swerved out of control to avoid hitting a young woman who was wheeling a pram across the road. The car tyres screeched eerily, the wheels spinning out from the back end as the car lay S-bend shapes of melted rubber all over the road. Linda sped up behind the small green car, suddenly feeling a big adrenaline rush. The Police Patrol Car was dangerously sliding sideways up on two wheels. Kirsten radios Shane for backup. Instantly, he let fly verbally, adrenaline pumping through his veins. His muscular leg pushes down full-throttle on the accelerator of his Police Patrol Car. The Police Siren is blaring as he quickly joins in the Police Car pursuit, now positioning his Police Patrol Car right behind Kirsten and Linda, who are already in hot pursuit of the two Offenders. As the small green car nears the roundabout, the vehicle dangerously mounts the roundabout curb. The car went straight ahead as other drivers on the road hit the brakes and swerved instantly to avoid a collision. Seriously focused and still buzzing emotionally, Linda continues driving in rapid pursuit. Kirsten subtly glimpsed sideways at the lake. She loved running around and wished for a moment that that was what she could be doing now instead of her present situation. Shane's voice echoes clearly over the radio. Shane, swearing and stressed, arrogantly starts instructing Linda how to drive. Linda ignores him at first. He started yelling uncontrollably on the radio. Kirsten, surprised, listens to Shane shouting over the radio. The next minute, Linda, known for her very Australian vitriol vocabulary, speaks into the radio powerfully, "Who the hell do you think you are... mate?" Kirsten just stared ahead, preferring not to buy into the drama. The stoplight turned red at a fast pace as the green car drove straight through it. Next minute a great white truck came out of the T-junction turning into Edwards Street. The young Offender driving, breaks too late. The green car's front wheel clipped the front of the big Truck. Its wheels seized up, and the car flipped and rolled over and over on its side due to the sudden impact. The green car landed upright and out bolted the two young offenders. The Truck suddenly stopped, blocking the way through for the Police Patrol Car and their vision of what lay ahead. Linda had mounted the curb to avoid slamming into the Truck. Shane spontaneously hit the brakes and crashed into the Stobie pole as there was no other way he could avoid driving into the oncoming traffic without causing a fatality. The two young Offenders had made a swift execution from the damaged green car. Escaping on foot amidst a dramatic scene of commotion, smashed vehicles, trauma victims, and three very frustrated Police Officers.

Shane angrily leap-ed out of his Police Patrol Car, rushing out to join Kirsten and Linda. His handsome face flushed with anger. The adrenaline rush was engulfing his muscular body and once again abusing Linda. Linda listened for a split second, then shut him down with her assertive masculine-sounding voice, "Get a grip, get over and assist those people, names and addresses are what you need, save the emotional barrage." He stared intensely, then buttoned his lip, knowing she was more senior in the ranks than he. Kirsten said nothing and remained serenely composed. Linda competitively looked at her, then said, "We're going after 'em, babe." The two women jumped back into the Police Patrol Car, siren screaming at top decibel. Linda sped off straight ahead, instinctively relying on her intuition to trace the whereabouts of the two young offenders, darting in and out of random streets at a rapid, reckless pace. Linda spontaneously hit the brakes, pulling over into the curb and giving one the impression that she was ending the chase. Linda abruptly turned to Kirsten, "What the hell is wrong with that misogynous bastard?" Kirsten sat calm and controlled. Turning to Linda, she calmly spoke, "I have no idea." Linda stated, "Shame we can't blame the Man Flu, huh?" "Mm," murmured Kirsten, agreeing with a cheeky grin. "He needs to pull his head in, Kirsten. Does he forget? We are more Senior to him. Even though you and I are on mutual ground with our ranks, Shane does not have the right to dictate rules to either of us or be disrespectful to women in the workplace. Hmmm?"

Linda slowly drove off from the side of the road back

into the mainstream traffic, becoming more aware of the surroundings. Realizing they were in the typical old industrial area of Reservoir. In the street were a few overly large, dilapidated, old, deserted warehouses. They stood abandoned a very, very time long ago.

Kirsten stared out the window, contemplating how the upcoming night with Shane would pan out. Given his present state of mind, how, and why was he changing so much, it became so disheartening. She knew deep down it was the effect of the steroids he was taking for that goddamn bodybuilding contest. She admired his commitment, consistency, and dedication to hard training. Kirsten was, after all, a mad fitness fanatic herself. Kirsten was totally against drugs of any sort, as she was so aware of the effects they can have on the user and the people in the individual's sphere. Although deep in thought, Kirsten remained alert to the current state of affairs. Kirsten suddenly ordered Linda to halt. Looking ahead above the old, iron-high fence before them and to the right, they swiftly pulled over again in the patrol car and sat, observing what appeared to be a young male climbing up the side of a very tall, disused water tank. The young male manoeuvred himself skilfully through the opening of the galvanized iron wall from the second level of the old run-down warehouse. Linda and Kirsten sat regarding their prey. They discovered they had to enter the building around the corner to access the deserted old warehouse. They radioed the location details to the Police Headquarters. They swiftly drove off in search of the opening of the old run-down warehouse. Linda pulled over the Patrol Car further down the road when they were closer to the isolated, large, deserted warehouse. In stealth-like style, both women moved out of the stationary Police Patrol Car. Batons and guns were ready for a direct attack as they vigilantly pursued their prey further toward the deserted large old double-storey building, which displayed a dishevelled demolition sign boldly on the front wall. Suddenly, a surge through Linda's adrenals gave her the feeling of transforming into a superwoman. Her body tightened as she felt the energy rising within, giving her an added sense of strength as she prepared herself for war with the unknown. They quickly moved across the large expanse of concrete surrounding the huge old warehouse.

Two

The two women continued toward the front of the building, then quietly moving further toward the very eerie deserted steel structure that stood before them. Both in suspense, gracefully and precisely moving with stern stone faces, focused and deliberate in their mission. Armed and ready to retaliate to anything and anyone who might attempt to shoot, harm, or endanger them in any way, shape, or form. Kirsten, calm and focused, moved close to the large door that was slightly ajar, gun clenched in the air, ready to fire with a controlled calculating exterior emanating from her. All that she could hear was the loud thud of her heart beating.

Linda moved to the same side of the building as Kirsten, who was now visually checking up and down the outside of the building. Nothing apparent, except for dust and dirt. Linda sighed a breath of relief that Kirsten subtly acknowledged. Kirsten shifted her focus back to concentrate on skilfully passing through the slightly open door of the large old warehouse undetected. Once inside, Kirsten stopped for a split second, alert and listening intently for any movement or foreign noise that perhaps may not sound befitting to this foreboding situation. Linda then made a move, as quiet as a mouse, they both entered deep into the building. Kirsten whispered, "Stay down," as they both slid sideways through the next slightly unsecured doorway.

    The interior of the large old building was dark and eerie except for some light emanating from the opening of the door. The rays of light shone through small nail holes in the galvanized steel roof high above, forming a clear pathway of light exposing floating dust particles and old dismantled rusted foundry machinery which lay scattered throughout the big old warehouse. Slowly, the two women advanced, deeper into the building. Aware of every single noise. BANG went the door. The noise reverberated, echoing through the large old building. They both instantly ducked to the ground. Linda, covered with goose-bumps as her body shivered with the chill. In silence with only fixed stares regarding one another, Linda was now unsure of their next move. The door opened ajar again. BANG went the door. Kirsten took charge, they moved quickly to the old wooden stairs, crouching down under them, Kirsten's mind calculating what to do next, the door BANGED loudly again. The timber supporting the galvanized iron shook frantically. Kirsten looks at Linda, whispering, "It's only the wind." Kirsten silently pointed to the stairs. They both knew instinctively what their next move was. Linda almost flew up the stairs, always in a hurry to conquer the quest, too curious to think about what danger may lay awaiting them. Kirsten calm stayed close to her, scanning every part of their surroundings, in front and behind as she knew only too often, how Linda, so addicted to the adrenaline rush, sometimes forgot to observe and anticipate another endangerment. Both crouched down to ensure they weren't detected they reached the top of the stairs. It was dark, creepy, and spooky with a powerful cold air of unexpectedness. The two kept moving forward through what appeared to be a small, isolated dark corridor. It smelt damp and musty. The stench of a dead rat wafted up Linda's nostrils. Linda had to hold herself back from dry-retching. They could hear the Police Siren screaming up and down the street. It sounded loud from where they now crouched, almost reverberating. Before them, a small corner appeared ahead in the building as they proceeded quietly forward to the top of the stairs. They came to a large open expanse of space. Subtle, gentle light shone through a hole in the roof, making the creepy unfamiliar surroundings pallidly far more visible.

Suddenly ahead of the two women, on an elevated segment giving the appearance of a platform, lay two teenage boys. Further away from them to the right, a young girl crouched against the wall in the corner, appearing to be in acute pain. Another teenage boy sat cross-legged on a box smoking what smelled like dope. They were unaware of Kirsten and Linda's presence. Linda, bombastic and impulsive, made a direct move headlong toward them. In the same breathe yells, "Don't move, any of you." Kirsten instantaneously backed Linda up, at the same time turning up the Police Radio loudly, Shane's voice coming over clearly. The Police Divvy Van pulled up out the front. The warehouse door aggressively opened on the ground floor. Chaotic noises came from downstairs. Shane and his other Police Co-workers bounded across the ground floor of the large old building and up the unsafe stairs, like a pack of wild banshees in hot pursuit of their prey.

The young blonde teenage girl in the corner was in her stoned head-space. Kirsten and Linda realized the flaccid teen girl was out of it by what appeared to be the effects of heroin. She was almost oblivious to what was going on in her present reality. She was in a bad way. Linda grabbed the young girl's skinny arms to handcuff her. She was waif-thin and smelt revolting as she hadn't showered for a while. Her baggy old black jumper was ragged and hung like a sack over her skinny body. Her jeans were ripped and filthy. Her designer desert boots appeared a size too large, with the toes worn out. The young girl was in a sweat and shaking. Some of her long blonde locks were drenched and matted. Kirsten's guess was she was approximately 15 and a bit years old.

Linda brutally dragged the young girl up as hard as she could, but Kirsten detected there was a subtle softness in Linda's voice as she questioned the young girl,

"What's your name?" "Tash," the moody girl replied. "Well, Tash," Linda said, "I hate to say it, but you look like shit, and you stink."

Tash was in a different dimension altogether. In her reality, she thought she was on a merry-go-round, spinning, feeling that her spirit was half out of her body and disconnected in her austral body. In Tash's head, everything was moving in slow motion. On staring at Kirsten, the young girl thought an angel's face had appeared before her. Tash was still mesmerized as Linda firmly led her down the stairs and out of the building, then loaded her into the Police Divvy Van.

The other two teenage boys stood braced in the presence of Shane, Kirsten, and other Police Officers. One struggled to set himself free of Shane's grip but to no avail. Shane was so strong compared to such a skinny runt of a boy, who would have only been about 12 or 13 years old with an enormous amount of grit, especially even contemplating taking on someone like Shane. Paul, one of the other Cops, laughed at the situation in almost an endearing way, knowing that physically the boy was in a no-win position. One teenager sat on one of the big wooden boxes. Unnerved by the whole scene and the intrusion by the law enforcement Officers. He was also pretty stoned, the unnatural state of bliss evident in his eyes. Kirsten feeling there was something different about him compared to the others. Something extremely calming and philosophical. His relaxed mood, perhaps accentuated by his substance abuse. Kirsten decided she would escort him downstairs. She handcuffed him. Without a struggle, he placidly vacated the scene along with Kirsten.

Last but not least, the third male, a tall gaunt, thin boy of about 15. He looked like a Gothic Vampire, as though he had a deadly illness, almost as if he were about to drop dead at any minute. He looked like a Junkie with a cough that sounded very toxic. His track-marked gangly arms made a blatant statement. His mind, lost in space and a ravenous temper, despite his apparent physical weakness. He aggressively fought and struggled with the other three Police as they dragged him out of the large old building, spewing forth bitter contempt and vulgar obscenities directed at the Police, While strange beings supposedly surrounded his physical space. The Police Divvy Van now loaded up with all the young Offenders then driven back down the road to the Police Station.

The four young Offenders were under arrest, which was perhaps in some way controversial. It may be difficult to lay charges due to the ages of the kids. They were locked up outside in the holding cells at the back of the Police Station. The Sergeant ordered that they be sprayed down, clothes and all, with a great deal of water and disinfectant, to rid them of the repulsive smell that emanated from them all. Anyway, it was summer in Australia, it would only take five minutes for them to dry off, so it didn't pose any threat to their health. It was apparent they hadn't showered in a very long time. Writing up the paperwork after the kids confessed to the crime was a job and a half. They were all street kids with no fixed addresses and with very dysfunctional backgrounds. All were reluctant to identify their parents. Locating the parents or any next of kin was going to be a task and a half.

The Police hashed the situation over among themselves for an hour or so, then deciding the way forward was to leave them in the cells overnight. Then in the morning, the Police would put the teens up before the Juvenile Aid Panel, who would have more information on where to fit them into the system. The Police weren't able to detain them for too long in the cells due to their ages. So now it was left to fate and the Judicial System.

Kirsten and Linda, exhausted, decided to wrap it up for the day. Linda, now in the change rooms changing into civvy clothes, packed up her gear in the locker, went back into the Police office to her desk to collect a few things, bade goodbye, stating short and sweet, "I'm out of here." to her Police co-workers, then left abruptly.

Kirsten sat at her desk quietly debating what her next move regards Shane would be. Shane sheepishly strolled up to her, "Will I see you tonight?" Kirsten nodded and started collecting some of her things along with some paperwork she had to collate for tomorrow's Court Session. Then she was about to leave the office, and she stopped for a moment.

"Oi Shane," called Tommy from across the other side of the office. Tommy was one of the other Cops on their Team, "You owe me twenty bucks. My Team won the footy, see mate, and you can't beat the Vics. They were bound to win the finals." The three verbally tussled over their footy teams, leaving the office to quickly gather and train down in the Police Gym. The Sargent came into the Office, Kirsten now the only one left in the office area. "How's it going, Kirsten? You handled the job well today." She smiled and replied, "Thanks, Sarge, just another day at the office. By the way, Sarge, do you think you could check on one of the teenage boys out in the lockup tonight, during the shift? I feel he's pretty sick." "Yeah, no worries," replied the Sarge, "Is he faking, though?" "No, I wouldn't think so, Sarge, not with a cough like that." "You might need to get a Doctor in or something. He appears to be in pretty bad shape." Kirsten looked at the Sarge compassionately, "O.K. I'll take your word for it. I'll see you tomorrow." She nodded respectfully, and trusting him, she left the office.

Three

Kirsten went from work straight to the gym and was glad of that as a stress release to attain some emotional balance. After an hour and a half of running, climbing, cycling, and working the abs, she felt the need to go home, sweating profusely and happily bidding farewell to the Gym Receptionist.

Returning home entering her front door heading straight for the shower. As she undressed and moved under the warm running waterfall from the shower, the feeling of peace washed over her entire being. The doorbell rang twice, and she heard the front door close then. Shortly after, Shane entered, "Hi, babe! Where are you?" Kirsten called out in a warm tone, "I'm in the shower," Shane entered the bathroom, "Hey!" as he opened the shower door to kiss her, he was still in his sweaty gym gear and looked hot as. His skin was a bit red from overstaying his visit to the solarium as he was hell-bent on looking tanned up on the stage at the comp. He went out to the kitchen to put on the kettle. Kirsten shook her head, thinking to herself that she was aware his ego was rising profusely as much as she loved him.

He came back into the bathroom, Kirsten was waiting for him to say something about work, and then he slid the shower door open again. "I spoke to Linda about today when we were out on the chase Kirsten." "Oh yes," replied Kirsten, "and what did Linda have to say?" She said I was a prick.". Kirsten repeats, "ah-ha."

"I apologized to her. I know my behavior was out of line," he said. "Ah-ha," replied Kirsten again. "Boy, it's hot in here," he took off his sweaty gym singlet.

He stood there, pensively leaning on the shower side, with one hand on his hip. Kirsten turned to wash the conditioner out of her long red hair, which, when wet, hung down to her waist. He was waiting for her to say something about the day.

"Kirsten, do you think I'm stressed? Perhaps I should take some time off work. . I experienced real anxiety. I've never had that before. Maybe I should go and see a Doctor," he proceeded then to sit on the side of the bathtub, taking off his shoes. Kirsten continued to shower as he sat there fixated on his issue and the dreaded feeling of anxiety he had felt. Standing up again, he said, "you're a nurse, what do you think?" He stuck his head into the shower alcove to kiss her cheek. He was sweating again, commenting once again how hot it was in the bathroom. He kissed Kirsten on the lips, running his fingers through her long wet hair. Moving into the shower, still half-clothed. Tenderly and passionately kissing her on the back of the neck, one of Kirsten's definite erogenous zones, as he moved downward, kissing her body, at the same time removing his tracksuit pants, then threw them over the top of the shower to land in the bathtub. They both laughed as he kissed her passionately between asking her what she thought. He grabbed the shower gel and soaped her sculptured toned body as the atmosphere ignited with the passion and entwined the two in the intense sensual energy that engulfed them both as he lifted her slippery feminine body up, pulling her into his groin. He was just about to enter her when in the kitchen his mobile rang loudly, Kirsten with a smile quick to state, "there goes your phone," "Don't worry about it," he said not wanting to spoil the moment, he was too aroused to want to stop now. "No, you're on call with the SOS tonight, remember?" said Kirsten. "Oh shit," Shane replied. He grabbed a white towel and ran to the phone in the kitchen. Kirsten turned off the shower, got out, put on her white toweling robe, and went out into the kitchen. Shane was angry. The hostile atmosphere was rising rapidly in the room.

Kirsten listened at the resonance in his voice as he on the phone, "What," he snapped, "tonight," he snapped again, "Now, you mean, Sarge?", still with a strong, angry resonance to his voice, "Fine," he grunted, ending the phone conversation, he sulkily threw the mobile on the couch. "I have to go to Thredbo. There's been a landslide, and I have to go to help out the Special Operations Group. There are twenty people trapped under a couple of Ski Lodges that collapsed. I have to go because they need more helpers from Interstate. What did the Sarge tell me I have to go for? Surely Tommy can go? I've got two weeks until the comp, the bastard. Why does he have to upset my life and my goals?" Kirsten boiled the kettle and started to cook some veggies and pasta for tea.

"Well, Tommy's not as good as you at search and rescue,

plus his wife is about to have her first child any hour now, plus last but not least, you can be recalled at any time, that's the job." Shane banged his fist on the kitchen bench, "Oh well, I don't fricken like it." Kirsten looked at him with empathy, he turned on the TV and loaded in the video, and he sat in his anger, watching the show sulking. Attempting to shut out the world.

Kirsten continued to cook dinner, which didn't take long. "Hon, dinner's on the table if you want something," he turned to her and said, "I don't want anything to eat," continuing to watch the footy show repeat, it was only Thursday, and Shane felt it was the end of the week. Shane had been through the mill. Now he had to go out and stay out all night on some ski slope in the cold, looking for many dead bodies. Not only that, he now had to miss out on being on duty at the Shopping Center for the filming of the Footy Show, where some of the special guests were members of the Port Footy Team, his favorite team. Shane felt his nerves were overtaking him. He sat back and took a deep breath. He suddenly felt a sharp pain in his heart, "oh my God," he felt light-headed and tried to breathe deeply. Kirsten observed him while eating her dinner from the table.

"Kirsten," he said, his voice became shaky, "I don't feel right." Cool and calm, Kirsten responded, "If I was that angry, I wouldn't either." He started breaking out in a sweat. He sat forward and bent over as he began to dry retch. Kirsten moved quickly toward him, grabbing a towel and passing it to him. "What the hell is wrong with me," he repeated, "What's wrong with me?" His whole body started to tremble and sweat. Kirsten half knelt beside him with one arm around his back,

"Hon," she said, "it's the steroids. They're not natural. I've seen this all before with Patients I used to look after. This is the start of the damaging effects it's having on your body." "Oh rubbish, I'm too tough for that." Kirsten looked at him with a strong sense of knowing. She was an intelligent woman who was well educated in the medical field and knew the signs. He stood up instantly, snapping, "I'm leaving. Goodbye." He walked out.

Kirsten sat there, watching him stride down the hallway of her old stylish Victorian home. He banged the front door shut behind him. As he vacated the house. Tears welled up in her eyes. She knew the relationship had taken a bad turn. As much as her love was trying to hold it together, she could feel the distance growing between them, and Shane's personality was becoming the duality of a pendulum swing.

Four

Kirsten arrived in the Police Office. It was 6.30 am. She was as reliable as the clock and as bright as usual. "Hi guys, how was the shift?" Met with a friendly response from all three cops sitting around the desk, her perfume emanated throughout the office. Her warm, feminine presence was felt by them all. She was a very popular character on the job. Tommy stated, "Shane's not too impressed. They radioed in during the night. They had to start work on arrival." Tommy said, "Have a look at this shit. As he pointed to the Television, the Press is really onto this. They've been giving an all-night visual account of the landslide." Paul piped up, very keen to advocate his services. He prayed one day Kirsten would actually notice him. "Would you like me to come to Court with you this morning? The Doctor was brought in at 3.00 am for that boy out in the Cells, the Sarge reckons the boy's got AIDS." Kirsten took one look at Paul. The Sarge emerged from his office, "Hi Kirsten, did the guys give you the rundown? Before everyone arrives for Parade, what do you think we should do? Let's hope he doesn't spit on us," and I mean that without any prejudiced sarcasm, we've got to take this into account, you know how feisty these teenagers are. We'll have to take all necessary precautions and find out from the Doctor what's happening with the blood tests. I went through enough emotional shit with everybody on the Team when John the Cadet killed himself after being jabbed by an infected needle. I wouldn't cope with that again. I'm too busy at the moment."

The Teens are all up before the Court first thing in the morning, and it was up to the Judge to decide what would happen next and where they would be placed, which would be somewhere safe in the Community. Kirsten went out straight after Parade to check on the teens. She gave Tash an old comb she'd found in the storage room and ordered her to comb her hair. Kirsten thinking to herself what a difference a simple thing can make. The young teen Tash was gorgeous. They all looked much better in appearance due to the shower, and for sure, the disgusting smell of body odor had disappeared. The teens were all put into the Police divvy van and driven to Court.

Kirsten had all the reports ready for the Juvenile Aid Panel, although she'd had her work cut out for her, trying to locate information regarding background checks for these street kids. They were first in, the Court was closed and emptied due to the ages of the teenagers.

Paul and Kirsten organized all the information on the Court desk to present to the Judge. The teenagers sat together, whispering between themselves. Linda emerged, at last, she bowed her head to acknowledge the Court Reporter and other Authorities as she entered the Court Room. Luckily for her, the hearing hadn't started. Kirsten could smell the faint smell of alcohol emanating subtly from Linda's breath. Paul moved close to sit next to Kirsten. Linda turned to him, "You right there?" she gave him that bear-down look of displeasure that made men very wary of her. Paul whispered sarcastically, "you been out on the piss again with the boys?" "Yeah," she snapped, her voice changed, "Oh, guess what Kirsten," with a cheerful tone, "Tommy's wife had a boy," trying to keep her voice low key as the members of the panel had now begun to enter the Court to take up their positions. The onus now switching to the teens seated before them who were about to be tried.

The sound of silence was momentarily deafening to the four teens sitting awaiting the verdict. It was inevitable that their reins would be pulled in severely, and they would lose their freedom. Although life had taken a twist for them, who knows where the road would lead. They certainly didn't have anything else planned at this point other than keeping their drug habits alive and supported. Zak's heroin habit, in reality, had taken him into his death wish now he knew for sure he had HIV. There was no turning back for him, and deep in his heart, he felt sad that this was all he had amounted to. He thought perhaps if his mother hadn't had such an addiction and taken the shit, that possibly his life would be very different. The habit was already bred into his genetics the day he was born. The last memory he had of his mother was as he crouched with her as she lay dead near a gum tree on the footpath.

Only three years old, Zak knelt beside her, kissing her hand, pleading and crying for her to wake up. Terrified he called for help. In his mind, Zak called for help but didn't know who to call to or what to say. After all, he was only three. Zak didn't know how to pray. Then the ambulance arrived and took away his mother, he never saw her again. The Police took him, Zak recalled they were good to him, then the welfare people collected him and so continued an even more intense traumatized dysfunctional childhood. The drugs created a fantastic psychedelic fantasia and a beautiful form of escapism that assisted as a tool to block out the emotional pain of the child battering and continued sexual abuse as he grew into his teens.

Occasionally he'd drop a bad trip, and it would bring up the nightmares that were confronting. He'd have to almost OD on ecstasy before the horrible visual distorted memories would disperse back into another realm of his mind. Deep down, nothing for him could ever take away the grief and sadness of being a little child left all alone, afraid, unloved. Completely abandoned, sitting in the gutter wondering what had happened to his mother, wondering if she would come back to get him. All this time he had spent existing but hadn't made the time to move past the anger of it all emotionally. So far, he had spent his life living in his negative belief systems and creating more based on the same mindset. Forgetting to realize he could choose to live differently and feel differently if he only could confront the pain and know how to start his healing journey. All it would take was his strength, but alas, he never took that option to face it because of the fear.

Grounding himself back into his present reality, he now knew that his future was now again decided by the authorities that had no emotional attachment to him whatsoever. They would deliver the law straight from a book as if the four of them were just absolute numbers that contributed to making up the darker side of Australian Society. He felt the grief of knowing that maybe he was once again about to lose his only substitute family, his only three friends sitting next to him in the Court pew. It had been the only bonding he'd experienced since living on the streets. In his distorted reality of coming down from his drug addiction, he felt anxious, which he tried to mask.

Judge Benetton sat listening to all the evidence, he was a mighty figure in the Community today, and it appeared to Kirsten he had lost a lot of weight. Kirsten had had dealings with him quite a bit over the years, primarily where Juvenile Drug Offenders were concerned, but there was a different look about him today as he stared down on the teens.

On hearing all the evidence, the Judge then spoke, focusing directly on the youths regarding their situation and then asking them individually how they each pleaded. The teens all knew there was no getting out of it. The only option being to plead guilty. Then there was the decision to be made as to where the youths would be sent. The Court adjourned momentarily for the Jury to decide over the options and to discuss with the Social Worker.

Returning to the room, the Jury quickly and methodically arranged themselves back in their seating, handing the Judge a written final decision.

The monotones were distinctive with clear diction, precision, and authority, which resonated throughout the dead silent atmosphere in the room. The four had been placed on Bonds and sent to a new facility for Homeless Juvenile Offenders. It was a relatively new trial scheme the Government had established as an alternative to the Remand Center System. There perhaps Zak's health could be restored in some way or at least improve a fraction. Daniel seated silently fixed next to Zak, bearing a great look of surprise on his extraordinarily handsome young face. Daniel had felt for sure he'd be imprisoned in the Remand Center. He almost collapsed with relief as he instantly relaxed on learning his fate.

Judge Benetton had been responsible for setting up this Scheme supporting and assisting young, reformed drug offenders by improving and motivating them through a rehabilitation process so they could progressively get their lives on track. Being an avid campaigner, Judge Benetton constantly sought the Australian Government to authorize the heroin program scheme. This had been very successful in Switzerland, significantly reducing the crime rate by half and preventing innocent people in Society from becoming victims of prey due to crimes committed by repeat drug offenders.

Kirsten hoped for these kids that something good would come from being sent to this place. Perhaps it would help in some small way. As everybody adjourned and the teens were led outside to the Police divvy van, Paul turned to Kirsten, "Hey, I'm a bit skeptical. What do you reckon? I hope there's good security in the place. No doubt the Judge would have made sure of that, from what I can gather, he has quite a bit to do with this Juvenile Facility." The next move was for Kirsten, Linda, and Paul to drive the teens to this new Juvenile Institution destination. On arrival, the teens were fingerprinted, interviewed by the staff, and as many details were taken as possible.

Kirsten, Linda, and Paul left the Juvenile Facility. They'd

completed their job at this point, so it was back to the Police Station. Linda jumped in the driver's seat, started up the engine, picked up the radio to notify the station they'd be back shortly. While they were driving around, Kirsten started to relax. She turned the radio on, switching channels to FM only, to be greeted with the very sudden shocking News that the Princess had been killed in a horrendous car accident in Paris while being pursued by paparazzi. The three cops glanced at each other in dismay. Linda, speaking abruptly, "Shit," she pulled over quickly to get the News. Paul now saying, "Christ, that's so sad, she was such a great ambassador for her country, incredibly humanitarian, and kind to the sick, God that will rock the world."

Kirsten sat for a minute in deep contemplation, "Just imagine working through all that emotional turmoil to finally become happy in oneself, then bang, dead in a matter of moments. How tragic, the devastation her two children must feel in their hearts." It triggered off issues regarding Kirsten's present relationship dilemma because she knew more than anyone that life could be so very, very short.

The three arrived back at the Police station. It was lunchtime. Linda asked around, "Anyone for Bergers?" a reply came from a couple of the guys. Linda loved the food, definitely addicted to it, she collected everyone's lunch money. Kirsten went out to the staff room. She opted for her Vedic diet, which, combined with her training program, helped keep her very balanced and in a healthy state of well-being. Balance was a requirement for the job and often challenging to maintain in certain circumstances when dealing with the raw emotions of traumatized people within the Community at times.

As Kirsten entered the staff room, Tommy called out to her, "Yoh, Shane rang you. He has to stay for the rest of the day. Apparently, there is a survivor. Some Ski Instructor is buried alive under the rubble at Thredbo. The CFS, and Emergency Service are working diligently to rescue the guy. He's trapped under four huge slabs of the concrete, poor bastard. The Press is really onto the case in a big way. So far, sadly, there's quite a few dead."

Kirsten knew Shane would have been working relentlessly to help the Rescue Team. She missed him and felt strange grief in her heart for him. She had hoped he'd return in a much better frame of mind and that they could talk about their relationship. Kirsten had decided that if they couldn't communicate and resolve the issues, then it would be best for them to part. They'd had some wonderful times together over the last three years, but the previous six months were agonizing since Shane had been on the steroids. His whole persona was changing. He'd gone from a beautiful, caring, loving being to a moody, irrational chauvinist. Kirsten knew she didn't need this kind of crap in her life, being very aware that while Shane was on the juice, he would only deteriorate, which would only create bedlam between them. The question was, how much was she prepared to put up with? Kirsten spent the rest of the day with the Sarge organizing a lot of mundane paperwork for near-future Court hearings and finishing off a Coroner's Report for another case. Sarge and Kirsten worked well together. Even though he was the boss, he depended very much on her, her intelligence, and the rapport she could establish quickly with almost every human being she came into contact with. The Sarge quietly respected her immensely but was also very aware of her incredible physical beauty and feminism. He often put that physical opinion aside to remain in his own professional and personal integrity.

He prided himself on having great respect for all women and was very fair to all his staff, no matter what caliber and genre. Kirsten and the Sarge completed the last task and wrapped it up for another day at the office. Kirsten bade farewell cheerfully and left. It was her roster-ed days off. She couldn't wait for some quiet time.

Kirsten had gotten up early to go for a jog around Edwards Lake. It was great, a little foggy, and quite deserted this morning. However, the change of air had moved to spring, and that was quite uplifting in itself. On returning home, she decided to involve herself in the garden of her little cottage to put herself in that meditative state connecting with the earth and nature. Quite often, this gave her alignment and clarity of thought. She shoveled the soil diligently, she turned on impulse, swiftly looking up to see who was casting the shadow on the ground before her, and to her surprise, Shane was standing there. Pensively and deep in thought, staring down at her. His perspiration shining in the noonday Australian sun. He kind of' looked a bit sheepish as he lent against the tank stand, rubbing his 3-day growth with one hand. Kirsten felt a strange, subtle quivering anxiety in the pit of her gut. She slowly walked towards him. He held out his arms to hug her, "I missed ya' babe." She reciprocated, "I missed you too... like a cuppa?" "That would be great," replied Shane, "can I just have a shower. First, I just had a quick workout on my way here. God, talk about a missed training session and so close to the comp." "OK, you do that. I'll just get the rest of the washing out on the line." Kirsten came back into the house walked into the bathroom. Shane was almost finished in the shower. "Babe, how about an early dinner date blended with an early night." "Sounds good to me," Kirsten felt that he was back into his good side. This was the real Shane. He came out of the bathroom dressed in a towel, looking hot, entered the living room, and switched on the TV. Kirsten entered freshly showered in her bathrobe and sat next to him on the sofa.

The News came on. The state's Nurses were striking, and Mother Theresa had died. Shane hugged Kirsten and kissed her on the head. Although he still hadn't apologized for storming out of the house and being such a prick, Kirsten, in the back of her mind, wasn't going to let him get away with it. At the moment, she was coolly biding her time, as she knew he hadn't slept for two and a half days to assist in saving that young ski. The instructor's life was, in itself, an incredible humanitarian thing to do.

As Shane relaxed into Kirsten's nurturing embrace, Shane started to drift off. He was so exhausted, his body's adrenaline was in overdrive, the footy results flashed on the screen, *"oh good, my footy team won, Tommy owes me $50."*

Kirsten watched her favorite show, 'Herculs,' feeling Shane should just sleep as he had an early shift in the morning. Part of her felt the grave disappointment of being let down, but understanding the pressure of the job. Two hours passed, Shane's mobile phone rang. Kirsten answered it. It was the Sarge. Waking, Shane found it hard at first to focus on the conversation after coming out of such a deep 5th rem sleep. "Mate, we need you to work tonight. The Casino has a big opening night for PL Hollywood. The crowds are going to be huge. There will be a lot of International and Australian Celebrities there tonight. We need your skills."

Shane's temper flared. He was becoming volatile. "Bullshit," Shane stated to the Sarge. "Mate, I'm sorry to do this, but that's the job. The Government has cut so much of the manpower. What else can I do?" "Sarge, I haven't slept for two and a half days. Give me a break." Shane sat on the couch, shaking his head. "I've got an early start in the morning. How's a bloke supposed to cope?" "Look," replied the serge. "You won't be finished till 2.00 am, so tomorrow, take that off in lieu," "OK, OK, alright," Shane replying with severe agitation. "We need Kirsten to be on patrol as well. Will you let her know? "Yeah, we'll be there at 2000 hours." Shane slammed down the phone. "We're on recall. What's the time, Kirsten?" "6:30pm," she replied. "We'd better get ready," Shane bitched. "No wonder the nurses and firemen at 6:30 pm went out on strike. Maybe the Police should go on strike. This is just bullshit." Kirsten knew that the docile lovable lamb had now turned back into the wild banshee from hell. Dressing into her uniform silently, she listened to him ranting and raving. The two left, called into the station to pick up their batons and guns and patrol car, clocked on and headed toward the city and Tommy, Paul, and Linda, who had all been recalled for duty. Kirsten was concerned. Linda had been called in while down the Police Club, having a few beers with the boys. She wasn't precisely prepped.

Kirsten felt the need to have a quiet talk with Linda about her drinking. She was hitting the booze a lot lately. Kirsten wondered if the stress of the job was getting to Linda or if it was the fact that she was just lonely and trying to prove something. Kirsten stayed close to Linda for the night, giving quiet support realizing Linda was slightly inebriated. If anything happened, Kirsten would have to take action and was switched on to take charge for both of them. It was a difficult night all around being on patrol as the crowd was huge, loud, and restless for hours.

Five

Marion sat sternly behind a large regal desk situated in the middle of a somewhat sophisticated masculine-looking office, displaying a superior sophisticated cold expressionless face. A definite hard power control freak. John, Tash, Daniel, and Zak, lined up in a row. None of them game to move, not even John the youngest. A 13-year-old with the most defiant rebellious nature dared to make a sound. Tash felt goosebumps climbing up her arms. She felt the woman as good looking as she was, was pure evil in itself. Tash deep down felt that if things got too bad, she could run home to her very rich, political high profile parents. Tash could always emotionally blackmail her father into anything, but there was no way at this point she would leave this adventure for the first time in her 15 years of existence. She felt immensely in love with Daniel. This mixed with an ecstasy and speed addiction stemming from her complex insecurities of unworthiness had caused her to maintain silence regarding her feelings for him. Daniel intuitively knew how Tash felt about him, but chose to avoid the situation, refusing to make any sexual moves having been brutally sexually abused as a child on many occasions in various foster homes. Daniel had learned a strong understanding of right and wrong in his heart, he loved her dearly as a friend with great protectiveness and loyalty, therefore, Daniel felt compelled to do the right thing by her and himself. He didn't want any emotional pain, that's why he enjoyed smoking dope so much, it numbed everything.

Standing on guard at the door were two six-foot humongous Security Guards, definitely a force not to be reckoned with, both standing silent, strong instance, hands crossed over across the front of their bodies, both bearing a significant small tattoo identical to each other, obviously some sort of emblem. Marion didn't appear to have one after all she wore white gloves which matched her classic Gray fitted suit. Marion spoke in a dominant husky voice laying down the law, of course, specifying various rules and regulations that must be complied with, while living within the walls of the Juvenile Institutional establishment. Notoriously the place was also now known for its hi-tech security technology equipment, yet amazingly enough, some of the Juvenile delinquents within had conceived a means of escape and unfortunately due to their drug addiction, were later found lying dead in the mall. There was no further need involving Police investigation, other than locating the biological parents, which in most cases seemed an arduously lost cause.

Then came very unexpected news, the four of them were to be conditioned and rehabilitated into normal living, to prepare them for living back in the community.

After having spent three days at the institution already carrying out various specified chores for the upkeep of the facility, being given new clothes, good ablution facilities for personal hygiene, the food extremely healthy, beds very comfortable.

Zak had been administered with massive doses of IV Chinese herbs and vitamins over the last couple of days, he'd almost dried out from his heroin addiction and in five days was to be put on emerge, an unlisted prescription drug that has minimal side effects and had been used over the years in Europe for heroin addicts, instead of weaning them off via the Methadone Program.

Just in such a short space of time, the lesions on his arm seemed to be dissolving, his mental reality was changing, his emaciated face started to have a tinge of a healthy glow. He did have severe cramps in his guts throughout the day, stemming from withdrawal, but the on-site Doctor had administered medication enabling the intense pain to subside considerably.

Zak was very suspicious of this whole setup, even though the tight security and strict staff were eminent. There was more to this, there had to be when things feel too good to be true, they usually were in his books. Zak was relieved to be getting a lot of medical help with his AIDS disease, although since contracting the deadly virus, he had not waive-red emotionally from his deeply ingrained world owes him syndrome, which would take a phenomenal amount of work.

A certain part of Zak was happy to receive help from the confines of the institution, though deciding to remain guarded, while slowly secretly planning his escape, refusing to be dictated to by any form of hierarchy.

Marion proceeded to give the four teens specific

instructions. They were actually to be chaperoned to the movies. Vicky was assigned to them for the outing, a peroxide attractive blonde, who had the faint look of anorexia, at first sight, you could see her soft side, mixed with vulnerability, then came the very hard 'I've lived on the street don't mess with me' dual persona. It was almost as if she'd been a street kid addict who grew up in the system and crossed the line to become a high-ranking Security Guard in the same Juvenile Institutional system. As she opened the door, John went to kick her and run out, her movements were with swift precision. Her hands instantly went on alternate sides of his throat, she grabbed his shirt collar so hard, deliberately setting out to choke him. John froze, man what a grip this woman had. "One flick of my wrist mate and you're dead, sad thing is, no one would even notice you after all a homeless person of no fixed address, do I make myself clear?" John's skinny little body broke into severe sweat, his heart pumping overtime with the onset of the extreme anxiety, trying hard not to disclose his fear, the other teens froze in their tracks. Vicki staring John down, let go instantly. John, still reeling in extreme anxiety, as the huge feelings of gloom crept into the dimensions of his emotions, his inner self knowing something was wrong here.

They were driven in the big clinically clean station wagon by a plain-clothed Guard, along with Vicky, the four teens were ordered to sit quietly in the time zone area. Tash loved these machines, each teen was given money to participate in specific games.

John slyly hid some of the coins as safekeeping, fearfully

hoping no one would notice, at least it was some form of backup for when he made his escape.

The four teens excitedly huddled around a space machine, engrossed with, "The Wishman Game," all teens now heavily in combat to win against the alien group of faction enemies against 'The Wishman' and Superhero, who was chosen by the Intergalactic hierarchy to protect Earth and help to bring peace across the Galactic Universe.

Very close by to the teens stood an onlooker, Zak glanced out the side of his eye, feeling the cold invasion of the guys' presence. At first Zak thought he may have been checking out Tash, after all, she was pretty hot. She'd scrubbed up well since living at the Juvenile Institution. Before that she'd just looked like a homeless grot. He sized up the stranger, as the stranger moved in closer to the four, Zak sneakily nudged Daniel, who replied, "yeah mate," in his soft charismatic Australian drawl. Zak with swift eye movement shot glances to his left in the stranger's direction. John also becoming aware, fully attacking in irrational defence mode, he blurted directly to the stranger, "what do you want?" Tash sitting in the space machines' driver's seat, completely immersed in the game of saving Earth, suddenly made aware of the strangers' presence spun her head, acknowledging her present surrounding reality. The bald trendy stranger leaned forward to shake Zak and Daniel's hand, the strong exotic aroma of aftershave wafted into their space.

Zak's unseen attention shifted, noting the strangers' left hand bore that same strange, unusual small round tattoo, trying to distinguish its design, one could almost identify its similarity to a Yin Yang Symbol.

The strangers' voice, masculine, with impeccable direction, "I thought you guys might like these four tickets to see the Movie "Shone", the session starts in 5 minutes."

John, being the little cheeky hustler, "What's the deal mate?" The stranger laughed at John's phobia psychosis. "I won them, but I didn't have anyone to give them to, so there you go, do you want them, or not, if you don't, I'll pass them on to somebody else." Tash grabbed them, "We'll take 'em," Tash and Zak viewed the Guard at that instant, who distinctly and discretely nodded his head. Off they scuttled, through the queue flashed the tickets at the Cinema Usher then entered the dark Cinema. Stopped by the female usherette, who then rechecked the tickets, John's paranoia rose again, thinking momentarily that they would be kicked out, the usherette politely stating, "Follow me please," as she made her way to the very top of the stairs, directing the four teens with her torch to their seats.

Daniel sat down, first letting out a sigh of relief, "Oh, cool, great view babe," speaking to Tash, who was desperate to sit next to him, as he put his arm around her in a nurturing fashion. Zak and John moved past Daniel taking up the next two seats. The Cinema up the back end contained quite a gathering, the front row seats below were vacant.

Tash gently trying to nuzzle in closer to enjoy Daniel's hug. He felt ok with that, after all, they were in the movies, nothing could happen. As the enjoyment of such a greatly crafted Australian movie came to a close, Tash had tears in her eyes, the first time she had such a release in a very long time. Tash reached down to grab a hanky from the knapsack, she didn't want the guys to see her vulnerability. Tash accidentally grabbed the leg of the guy next to her "ooh" came the expression, as she flinched back in her seat, startled in the dark. She touched him on the leg again, feeling its rock hardness, whispering "I'm so sorry, I was looking for my bag." A strong manly voice in the dark, showing no signs of flinching, stated, "It's fine." Confusion reigned within her. her thought her bag had been closer placed next to her. Tash started analyzing her thinking. Suspicion began to set in. Maybe he'd stolen something from her bag, it was filled with all her worldly goods just in case she had the chance to make a quick escape.

Tash travelled lightly on most occasions, sadly for all four, the movie ended, the lights subtly brightening. The Guard appeared from nowhere, leaning over speaking to Zak, "you guys ready?" Zak and John started moving up and out, they weren't arguing with a man of few words with such a huge physical disposition. Daniel coolly moved, turning then to grab Tash's hand, Tash so caught up in her illusion of a romance, followed Daniel's lead. "Oi, Miss." came a stern direct voice, as Tash moved past the couple next to her, taking one step down the stairs, she felt a tug on her lycra fitted top, resenting it being pulled, hostility instantly halting her in her tracks. Tash turned quickly about to verbally swear. In the dim lighting directly in front of her, sat a beautiful red-headed woman smiling. The woman looked so familiar; Tash couldn't place her. The man stretched out to her with his arm holding a bag, "Miss, you forgot you're backpack," backtracking instantly, she sharply responded, "Oh, I did too," she thanked him quickly as he handed over the bag, Tash hadn't realized how heavy it was until now, almost dropping such a heavyweight. Perhaps only now recognizing her own physically weak body strength, rather than her previous extroverted concept which had stemmed out of a drug-induced reality.

As they came to the bottom of the long staircase Daniel looked at her, speaking in his laid-back voice, "Temper, temper, see babe," Tash caught onto his gist, and laughing a little. Daniel endearingly shook his head. Such a peaceful soul, thought Tash.

Out in the foyer, Daniel let go of her hand before the Guard saw them together, silently, she felt instantly rejected and left drowning in her insecurities. Being streetwise, she knew that it was for her protection, a very honorable practical act by Daniel, Tash still in her childishness couldn't help but sulk. The four teens were ordered to leave the building and head toward the car park. Vicki's gravel voice yelled across the almost vacant car park, "Hurry up you guys, we'll be late back."

Kirsten got up from her Cinema seat, turning to Shane, "do you reckon that girl looked familiar?" "Yeah, kinda, I think she just wanted to play with my leg." Kirsten looking bemused, how typical of his blatant recent overly large ego. "I'm sure the boy with her was familiar as well." For a moment assessing her mind's process of memory recall. Shane and Kirsten then left briskly through the Cinema foyer, vacating the building, stepping outside. As they ventured to cross the pedestrian walkway a Police Patrol Car pulled up, it was Tommy and Paul, they pulled over suddenly and stopped to chat with Shane.

Kirsten focusing her observation on the four teens from the Cinema now walking toward the very thin authoritarian blonde woman standing next to the big station wagon in the car park. Kirsten's intuition spoke but became distracted by Shane pulling Kirsten close to him. Kirsten leaned down to greet both guys, they were happy to see her. "Good movie?" inquired Paul. "Exceptionally good for Australia," replied Kirsten very patriotically with a smile. "Kirsten, I'll drop you off, and then I'm going to train with the boys," said Shane.

Kirsten, completely caught off guard, knowing he'd already trained that morning said nothing, she felt cut-off emotionally, once again he'd let her down on the dinner date. She tried to hide her pain so as not to embarrass anyone or herself.

Shane was too caught up in his obsession to even notice. "Tommy, did the Vics win or did the Vics win? Once again mate, you owe me 50 bucks." Tommy directed the conversation to Kirsten, "We won't be training for long. I have to take Simone to the specialist, she's got post-natal depression. I don't want anything to happen to her, she needs my support." Paul looked forlornly at Kirsten, wanting to hug her. Tommy asked Kirsten if she knew much about post-natal depression, who answered as if straight from the medical journal itself that supposedly it was based on a hormonal imbalance and she needs to find a good counsellor to also help her through the process. Shane crassly stated, "That's what I must be suffering from, the imbalance of testosterone." "No," stated Paul stoutly, with the question in his tone of voice, "that's just too much of the juice. Aye?"

Tommy refrained from joining in on the banter, he was worried for his wife, he loved her so much and wasn't sure if Shane was taking steroids. "Meet you in five guys," replied Shane as he whisked Kirsten away.

The teens had now got into the big station wagon, the dark tinted windows automatically closing except for the drivers, which remained down, Vicki intense staring out from a distance she observed Kirsten and Shane as they walked toward their car over in the car park.

Kirsten, even in her dismal frame of mind, made a mental note of the big station wagon's number plate. As Vicki screeched the wheels and drove off. Kirsten slipped into the passenger seat of her car, writing down the number plate, curious to collect any data concerning the blonde woman, just to satisfy that detective mind she possessed.

Shane was speeding, Kirsten gently reminding him of the limit, he turned his head toward her with great audacity and sarcasm, replied "What are you gonna do, book me? yeah, yeah." He started to break out into an incredible sweat, his blood pressure rising profusely.

Kirsten looked straight ahead, in her mind now knowing it was over for her, she was sick of being a doormat, not at all deserving this shit, the inevitable was about to happen, Kirsten was going to end it now. He pulled into the driveway and hit the brakes, Kirsten got out of her little sports car, closing the door behind her, Shane immediately reversed out onto the road, beeping the horn, and sped off. Kirsten stood on the footpath in front of her home watching him drive away, feeling a huge hollow emptiness in her sad, sad heart. This was a very crushing moment, one she would remember for a long time, the emptiness so insurmountable. Kirsten slowly walked down the garden path, entering the little cottage, tears streaming like rain down her hauntingly beautiful face. She had now lost all hope that things would be better. Kirsten inwardly recognized that hope can be a dangerous thing sometimes. Moving to the living room, she forlornly turned on the stereo, switched it to tape, inserted her girlfriend's demo, appropriately named for this poignant moment 'Broken Hearts' by D, an Australian singer, who Kirsten met when nursing, they'd bonded instantly, one of those soul mate things. D's voice could always be heard hypnotically wafting through the old hospital like a nightingale, soothing the wounded souls and the sick. An incredible undiscovered talent who was destined for greatness, she'd made this tape for Kirsten's last birthday, it was of great sentimental value, it was also a parting gift when D returned to live in Sydney to sing in the stage play, 'JC Superstar' showcasing at the Opera House.

Kirsten lay on the sofa hugging the cream calico pillow, staring at the ceiling, tears flowing, absorbing the soulful words emanating through to her shattered broken heart. Kirsten felt alone, barren, and desolate. Emotionally exhausted, Kirsten drifted into a deep slumber. She felt trapped unable to even go out. Shane selfishly had taken her car, Shane had absolutely no concept of what was going on, completely obsessed by his ego, desperately fixated on wanting to win the bodybuilding comp at all cost.

Emotionally exhausted Kirsten drifted off to sleep. The phone rang loudly, echoing throughout the house, ringing for some time before Kirsten came around from such a deep sleep. The voice of Shane came over the line, vivaciously inquiring as to what she was doing. Kirsten glanced at the clock, it was now 9.30 p.m. "Listen, Sarge wants you here to do a strip search on this Offender the guys arrested, can you come now? Linda's too pissed to be recalled. Paul can drop by in the Patrol Car and pick you up, ok babe, he'll be there in 10. Where's your smile?" he cheekily commented, "See ya." He hung up, not even realizing Kirsten had picked up the phone and not even spoken a word. Kirsten was fired up as she entered the bathroom, quickly checking out her face, applying a lot of makeup to hide the puffiness caused by tears, applying eye drops to the eyes to take away the redness, not having alaot of time to get ready, opting to wear her current trendy casual clothes. In a heartbeat, Paul pulled up in the driveway in the Police Patrol car. Agilely moving out of the Police Patrol Car, walking with a quickened pace to the back door of the cottage, Kirsten greeted him, "Oh Paul, you should have come to the front door, so I didn't keep you waiting." He didn't care, the motive of going to the back was in fact in hope that he would be invited into her house. Once inside he felt consumed by the atmosphere of feminine beauty in her warm cosy quaint home. Feeling the urge to grab Kirsten and tell her he loved her, restraining himself imagining the rejection, he had his pride, although right at this moment he thought about throwing caution to the wind, however, restraint was very necessary. "Oh, ah, you're looking good," "Come on," she laughed at his comment, grabbing her handbag to leave, turning off the lights, they headed down the hallway. "Hang on a minute, I forgot something," Kirsten raced back to grab the scribbled number plate of that woman she had seen today while at the station, she'd do a check on the vehicle.

Arriving back at the Police Station within minutes, completing the delegated task, Kirsten went down to her desk, set up a computer check, discovering the vehicle belonged to Marion Goven, Head Administrator of the Juvenile Institutional Facility. "Mmm, interesting," now it fell into place, "the kids were the ones they'd arrested early on during the week, they certainly looked different in such a short period." Confused, Kirsten explained to Paul. Kirsten called out to the Sarge, "Did any of those lost teens parents match up to the street kids we arrested early last week?" "No, only the one we sent to the detention center for robbing that old woman, which reminds me, she asked me to give you something, I'll grab it for ya." As he came back out of his office, he tripped over the bottom filing cabinet that had been left out, falling to his knees, landing directly in front of Kirsten, cracking up laughing, but still holding a beautiful long-stemmed apricot rose in his hand, they both chuckled, all of a sudden he became serious, repeating the old ladies words of gratitude toward Kirsten's kindness.

Right at that precise moment, Shane appeared in the doorway, stopping dead in his tracks, instantly becoming overwrought with jealous rage unable to bite his tongue, "What the hell is going on?" he charged with the jealous aggression of a ranting bull, straight toward the Sarge, who almost fell over startled by the shock of Shane's reaction over such a trivial innocent thing. Paul and Tommy grabbed Shane, attempting to detain him, Kirsten, amid the scuffle walked assertively straight toward the men, who then stepped aside, aware of her forthcoming assertive presence, Kirsten planted the biggest king-hit directly on Shane's chin, almost knocking him unconscious. He and everyone else in the room froze in complete disbelief as to what had just taken place, the Sarge flabbergasted. No one spoke a word. The silence was deafening, you could have heard a pin drop, coldly staring at him in the eye, speaking in a very matter-of-fact voice, "We're finished."

No one spoke as she grabbed her keys and left the room, everyone staring speechless after her. Kirsten proceeded to clock off for the night, getting into her car and slowly driving home. Entering her warm cosy house, she banged the door closed on the world, walked into the living room, flopped onto the sofa, sitting there once again, staring at the ceiling, she felt emotionally drained. Hit by blatant obviousness the relationship was well and truly over. Consumed with the intense buckling void of grief.

Six

As the car drove down Settlement Road, Deep in thought, Daniel looked out the window, being unable to wind it down, noticing the small logo on the Window Payne bearing the words unbreakable glass. This was undoubtedly another imprisonment. He felt suffocated by their rules and strict regulation laws on speaking and not speaking, cleaning, and constantly working. What a crock of shit, he thought. He'd never felt so suffocated and the cold aloofness of these people. It was as though they were all tarred with the same scrupulous brush. Daniel questioned what had influenced these people to act like this, was it life, bad experiences, a false sense of power, or what?

He felt as a teenager that he would grow and flow along with life, you know, eventually be happy in a house with the Australian concept of the wife, a good job, the car, and 2 children. These people were already at this point in their lives, Daniel presumed, they would all have that indeed. Yet it appeared nothing like that at all. Their ruthlessness and cruelty were staggering. He hoped he never ended up being a barbaric adult like them. Maybe he thought to himself, they'd been through the same life traumas as him, no, they couldn't have, even though he'd had sexual abuse and beatings continuously throughout his childhood, he wasn't a bitter soul. Sure, he had his shit, probably a lot more issues than the average, but he could still laugh, give and receive love.

What's the big deal? Perhaps they needed a joke or two? Maybe they'd chill a little with their treacherous behavior. His mind drifted back further, almost to a strange land where he could distinctly fondly remember his dear adopted Foster Mother Ester. Often he could smell the faint enchanting scent of her. He had never had a more loving, caring foster mum. She was old, so he thought, but so caring. She took the time to explain to him anything he needed to know from a small child's perspective. She took the time to love him, always reassuring him how special he was, how important he was to her. Ester was a devoted Catholic, taking him often to church and charity fundraisers, a grey-haired, small, distinguished woman with a great deal of energy, a great cook, and many friends.

When he lived with her, they'd huddle around the fire at night together. She'd read him stories from the bible and fairy tales of strange, strange lands, one's she'd been to, to feed starving babies and nursing sick, dying children. Ester taught him about being wise and fair with human beings. Daniel remembered his 8th birthday distinctively. He'd slept in. Ester didn't come to wake him with his Hot Chocolate. That was something she always did. He ran into her room and jumped up on her four-poster bed. He bounced up and down giggling, singing Happy Birthday to me. Ester's eyes were shut tight. He thought she was foxing with him as she often did that. Ester's skin looked very, very whitish-grey in the sun. Daniel kissed her cheek and felt the weirdest sensation. She was frozen cold. Kneeling back on his haunches, he poked his finger gently in her eye. She didn't flinch.

He pulled up her eyelid, a cold fixed lifeless stare emanated from Ester's eye, his young body embraced her, trying to wake her. Still, to no avail, he knew there was something wrong, panicking. He started to cry, intuitively knowing she was dead, "Please God, please help Ester wake up, please," he pleaded, repeating it over and over again, almost in a chant-like fashion, but nothing happened.

Suddenly, thinking Jack the gardener next door might know what to do. He ran out of the house straight into the neighbor's house, screaming, "Jack, Jack, please help, can you help," bang, bang, bang on the door. Old Jack, a friendly stocky old guy, came to the back door, "hey mate, g'day, you forgot the rest of ya clothes, Happy Birthday mate." Daniel fearfully yelling, "Ester can't wake up, Jack, can you see." All of a sudden, Jack looked down very seriously over his half-eye bifocals. Reacting instantly, "show me, quickly," he said, the old man felt the gut retching inevitable, hurrying through the house to Esters' room, he knew straight away she was dead. He couldn't bring himself to tell Daniel, so he said, "Come on, son, we'll ring the doc." Jack inside was devastated, trying so hard not to show it, overwhelmed with compassion as to the future of such a young little boy and the loss of his dearly beloved friend.

The Doctor arrived checking out the scene, the complete bearer of bad news. Daniel sat huddled up on Jack's lap in the rocking chair, fearfully waiting for the verdict. Bluntly, the

Doctor made a short, direct statement stating Ester was dead, very matter of fact. Notifying the undertaker then signing the death certificate, he swiftly vacated the premises.

Daniel didn't understand what dead meant being only a child. He only knew when Jack said that she'd gone to heaven. And moved a very long way away. His little heart was so broken. Jack was a kind soul to Daniel, but the shock had blocked off many of Daniel's childhood memories of incidents over the next couple of days. Next minute it was as if he woke up in a church, in front of a coffin, with a young priest speaking to the people who had been at Esters for dinner lots of times. Daniel and he had kicked the footy around heaps out in the yard. Daniel, in his childlike confusion, thought he was going to live with Jack or the Priest, but as he sat on a stool in the church, the last of the crowd petered out, and Esters coffin had gone, the Priest took him by the hand, a Welfare Officer entered the church and took Daniel away. The Priest explaining to Daniel that he would be in safe hands, while all Daniel could do was weep, his little heart distraught with pain, indeed now a sad, sad little boy. Sometimes, while being so stoned, he had live conversations with Esters spirit, visualizing her and feeling her love with perfect memory.

As night drew close, every night in his new foster home, the man in charge of the house constantly and grotesquely sexually abused him in the dark, for nights and nights on end. Daniel lived for years with constant panic attacks in the pit of his gut and couldn't concentrate at school, nor could he eat properly. Choosing to shy away from being involved with other people. He quite often disliked the fact people were so magnetized to him and his handsome, good looks. If they tried to get too close physically or emotionally, he'd back off and start pacing, not understanding why he did that himself. It just made him feel safer and helped him release pent-up energy so he could calm himself.

Back in the moment, as the big station wagon pulled up in the driveway, the remote-controlled iron gates opened in synchronized fashion, then the roller door came up in perfect timing. Vicki smoothly driving the car inside, the car doors unlocked the Guard hoped out of the passenger seat. Security cameras beamed on them all. Even the cameras were synchronized. Vicki pressed through her card, coded in the pin, the thick steel doors instantly opened. Out the corner of his eye, Daniel viewed the code she'd put in, making a mental note of it.

As the roller doors started to close, John decided it was now or never, and in a fast twitching movement, decided to bolt. But just not quick enough, for the massive Guard who grabbed him by the back of the neck picked him up off the ground, walked inside the security doors, slamming John directly into the opposite wall. John lost his breath from the physical shock, his lungs ceased, going into a panic because he couldn't breathe, he fell to the ground lying flat on the floorboards, desperately trying to get his breath. He rolled onto his small thin back. As John moved over in synchronized movement, the Guard kicked him directly in the middle of the ribs. John sensed it coming, but couldn't protect himself quickly enough, then snap, the pain riveted through his body, John knew his lower rib was broken, he screamed in pain, clutching his side. The Guard ordered John to get up, gasping for breath, refusing to cry, scared of what would come next, he clutched at the immaculately polished floor of the corridor.

Lifting his head lethargically to see his three mates standing five feet away in disbelief and terrified at what they had witnessed. Slowly, on all fours, then using the wall to support himself to stand, he moved painfully up to try and regroup with his pals. John's body shook. The other three were too afraid to speak in case they too were victimized. All four were marched to Marion's office. John sat on the chair, deliriously in pain, cramped to one side, clutching his broken rib. He thought he was going to die as he struggled to breathe.

As Marion entered the room flanked by Vicki and another middle-aged woman dressed in uniform and wearing the mean look of a possessed venomous power-hungry woman, the four sat in silence. She was damn surly to boot, thought Tash. Tash's goosebumps rose on her arms, chilling her spine, freezing her steadfast in the chair. Marion sat down in her stately, arrogant manner, staring directly at Tash, who was unaware that she'd done anything wrong but feeling guilty anyway. Teenage rage swelled within her. "Give me that backpack." sternly, ordered Marion. Tash shaking reluctantly, handed it over. Marion unzipped the top, aggressively turning it upside down to disclose four substantial plastic bags filled to the brim. Undoing one, she stuck her finger in it, she bought her finger to her tongue and standing then leaning over changing her posture to a more dominant one stating, "mmm tastes like LSD, and this one, mmm cocaine." "What's that taste like to you, Tash?" grabbing her finger, sticking it in the bag, and forcing Tash to taste it. With incense surprise Tash was now terrified blurted out, "I don't know how it got there, honest I don't." Tash trembling, wondering how the hell that had come about, convincing herself this wasn't a dream, it was real life, shit, something like you see in a movie. Still, this scene generally didn't happen in Australia, nor had it happened in her life. It's real, which intensified her fear within.

Marion grabbed Tash by the throat, sarcastically mimicking Tash, "I don't know, I don't know." Marion's grip was almost like a vice, instilling further anxiety into Tash. As Marion threw Tash aggressively back into the chair, the chair abruptly rocked back and forth with Tash's rigid thin frame of a body pinned to it. Was she dreaming? Was this a hallucination?

Marion, now demanding, turned directly to the older surly uniformed woman," would you like to inform these teenagers as to the law on drug trafficking?" The four dumbfounded, looking at each other for answers, then looking straight ahead at a person stepping forward in uniform, the dragon from hell. Marion introduced her as Helen.

The four knew there was more to this than met the eye. Warily listening, not volunteering one ounce of emotion, it was explained to Tash and Zak that they could now be sent to jail for such charges as they had now breached their good behavior bonds. Soon they would be over and above the age of Juvenile Delinquents. Different laws come into play with the judicial system over the age of 16.

John and Daniel had no option other than to comply. Otherwise, they thought they might be killed. Daniel sitting in his chair, filled with dread, feeling that this was heavy shit and not his scene. He was getting out of this place somehow. He didn't know how, but he would get to freedom.

Helen gave a graphic explanation detailing gruesome accounts of some of the teenagers that had tried to escape the walls of the Juvenile institution establishment and their fate. Reiterating that they were members of 'The Golden Phoenix' now, representing a solid satanic cult, the staff members are all hierarchy members.

John's panic attack became so fierce, he began dry retching. He felt the four of them in his un- intellectual opinion were screwed. Helen cautioned them 'observe,' then switching to a powerful but weird space in her head, placing herself three feet to the right of Marion's desk. Helen ordered Vicki to stand ten feet opposite her in complete alignment and raise the gun to shoot. The Teens freaked, thinking one of them was going to be shot. Helen coldly stared at them, stating, "now you will see how powerful my mind is."Ordering Vicky to shoot at her, at that split-second, Helen emanated a dark, intense gravitational energy from her eyes, three feet before encountering her auric field, the bullet completely slowed down to time-lapse, moving caterpillar-like through the air. Her gaze was fixed. Projecting a dark, intense invisible shield controlling and slowing the bullet. raising her hand to grasp the very, very slow-moving bullet through the air coming at her, suddenly clasping her hand tight, she flicked her hand over to reveal the hot bullet. "Hmmm," she scoffed, her demanding ego rearing. "See how powerful my mind is." grabbing John aggressively, pulling him up from his chair then standing him directly in the firing line. He crumpled over in extreme pain, his face demonstrating mental torture.

John wasn't even able to comprehend that stunt, his mind racing questioning if that was humanly possible? Feeling so overwhelmed, knowing he did not possess such power to combat any bullet being fired at him. BANG, the sound was distinctively louder than the last. John hit the floor lying motionless. Vicki's laugh was ear piercing. Zak thought the laughter sounded to be on a parallel to a famous witch film. Vicki hysterically laughed continuously. Tash's eyes welled up with big tears, her lip quivered. Helen grabbed John's skinny little body and threw him back into the chair. See, fear has no fear but fear itself. She grabbed the glass of water from Marion's desk and threw it into his face. He moved slightly, Daniel looked again. His body relaxing suddenly, "Thank Christ, he only fainted," stated Daniel. Marion suddenly squeezed Daniel's face in her hand, "Don't ever mention that name in here again. Do you hear? That name is banned, now get out, the lot of you!" Daniel was somewhat perplexed but remained silent. Sized Marion up with a look. Tash was so relieved. John wasn't dead. What a draining emotional ordeal. They were ordered to return to their rooms and not to speak one word. John tried showering himself with difficulty, after laying on the bed looking up at the security camera, knowing he was constantly observed by somebody, but who was it? The feeling was eerie.

The Doctor entered the room who had come to fix John's wound and ribs. The Doctor was scrupulous. However, he didn't inflict any more pain while trying to splint John's now diagnosed broken ribs. He quietly also sewed up the small gaping wound in his rib cage. He gave John a shot of morphine. It didn't shift the physical pain, as his body was biochemically immune from his years of being a drug addict.

John lay there motionless, afraid to sleep, afraid to move, afraid to think. His mind running and distorted, grasping annihilation's of "What if." What had blown him away the most was Helen and that bullet. Was it just a theatrical stunt just to scare them, or did they have strong magical powers?

Seven

It was Sunday, Kirsten's was up early. It was a beautiful sunny day. She decided to go for a quick run around the lake, it was a blessing living a street away, and it was a better option than sitting around doing nothing but being depressed over Shane. Kirsten was definite. She had to move forward and heal from the ending of the relationship. It was going to take time and be a complicated emotional challenge. Kirsten was not one to fall in love easily, and she did love him so. She ran hard, completed the distance swiftly, and returned home for a shower. The water washed over her like a peaceful, soothing waterfall. She breathed deep and washed away all the negative thoughts.

Sitting in the kitchen dressed in her white bathrobe, eating her organic muesli at the kitchen bench, she sat pondering momentarily. It had been a long time since she'd been to church. Making an impulsive decision to go. She dressed and left to attend the local Catholic Church located in a beautiful old worldly setting. Large gum trees and willows stood boldly, branches swaying in the wind. The atmosphere of the gardens was quite inviting and peaceful on this beautiful sunny morning.

Kirsten entered the foyer of the old blue stone Historic building. Kirsten blessed herself with holy water, taking a seat in the old polished mahogany pew at the very back row of the church. A handful of people sparsely distributed themselves throughout the vicinity of giant statues of Saints and Catholic Antiquity. An Angelic voice aided by the music from the historical organ wafted throughout the atmosphere creating a peaceful, serene angelical ambiance. Kirsten had forgotten how long it had been since she'd been to a holy place of prayer, losing a lot of faith in religion after arresting a few men of the 'holy cloth' who'd sexually abused children. Disillusioned by it all, she'd felt her religious upbringing was somewhat a facade and thought that some of the people in these organizations were so radically hypocritical on occasion. The saintly music came to a lull as a Priest, Father Gibson ingressed up the aisle, heavily clad in elaborated priestly robes, he was indeed a handsome man in his very early 40's. He almost looked like Grantham Gibson, which was ironic, with the same surname. Funny how life presents itself sometimes. Delivering a profound sermon to a devout adoring crowd. His words surprisingly added some meaning to Kirsten's present reality, helping a little heal the pain of her broken heart, adding a little more strength and motivation with his warm words of wisdom. The members then disassembled. Kirsten sat for a while in meditative thought. Father Gibson stood at the doorway, warmly bidding people farewell. She felt it was time to go. As she turned to genuflect, Father Gibson was standing at the door about to come back inside. As Kirsten went to shake his hand to say goodbye, he put his hand on her shoulder, gently speaking to her. "You look troubled child," glancing at him surprisingly, "Hmmm, a little bit, but I'll be fine." "Was it something in the sermon?" he replied in his Irish twang. "Maybe," said Kirsten. "What's your name, child?" he inquired. "Kirsten," she stated, truncated. "Would you like to talk about it," offering his counsel? "There's probably not a lot to chat about." The Priest laughed endearingly at her comment. Walking her outside into the sunshine, sitting on the bench under the gum tree.

"Great day," he said. The cockatoo rustled itself in the tree, starting up into a screeching tone, singing the Our Father. Kirsten cracked up laughing, "Well, he's well trained." "Yes, that he is," replied Father Gibson. "So, what do you do for a living, Kirsten?" "I work for the Government." "What a stroke of luck," he replied. "Why?" stated Kirsten suspiciously. "Dear God, is there such great cause to be so defensive?" "Sorry, being a Police Officer can make you that way sometimes." "Well, in life, dear, it's not what the job deals you. It's how you deal with it. Not everyone's a bad guy, you know." His pale blue-green eyes emanated a soft, warm, nurturing energy. "Yeah, yeah, you're right," knowing intuitively he was coming from a profound spiritual space. Being quietly aware that, in the job, you can grow to mistrust constantly, you are on guard most times because it is often a case of survival. You have to watch your back and protect your co-workers, which can be a stressful dangerous position at times, but it is essential to always find a positive balance.

As they sat chatting and enjoying the moment, a carload of youths slowly drove past, beeping the horn continuously, leaving behind a trail of red, black, and white balloons, whistling and yahooing. "Hmmm, it's part of what you have to deal with all the time," stated Kirsten. "They're probably just getting over the Vic's loss against the Adelaide," replied the Priest. "It's an early morning start to the grieving process," replied Kirsten, "The truth be known, they were probably just coming home from the football game yesterday," chuckled Father Gibson. The two sat chatting about Shane and her recent breakup. Father Gibson gave her constructive information that he thought from a man's perspective might be of help. Engrossed in the conversation, the time flew by. Through the driveway appeared a little yellow car, out climbed a small bald orange-robed man, roughly at Kirsten's guess in his very early forties. Father Gibson introduced the man to her. It was his brother Bunta, a Buddhist Monk who ran the monastery down the road. Kirsten was invited to lunch with them. It was an interesting experience, discovering a basic understanding of the philosophy of Buddhist life over coffee and cake. Father Gibson raised the issue of the missing child that had been adopted out quite some time ago, a woman in his congregation was trying to locate this teenager, and Father Gibson and Bunta had been trying to help her. Kirsten piped up, "Father, you know there's a Juvenile Institution that we forward a lot of juvenile homeless delinquents to, so they're not living on the streets, the Government rehabilitates some drug-addicted youths in these places. There are two facilities I know off of hand, perhaps you could contact the Social Worker at each of the Juvenile Institutions, and maybe you'll have some luck." "Perhaps, Dear, that would be a marvelous idea." Bunta agreed, gently nodding his head, both being happy with a positive sign, giving one hope that this alternative may provide a solid lead for the teen's whereabouts.

Kirsten felt it had been an interesting afternoon, and being in different surroundings had given her more insight to move forward in her life. She was in a more positive frame of mind, and it helped a little to put the pain of her past relationship behind. Kirsten was realistic, she knew it would take time to heal the wounds of her broken heart, but she felt now that perhaps things may get a little better over time.

As she happily bade farewell to Father Gibson and the Monk, she casually mentioned to Father Gibson that she would help him if she could with his dilemma and left them there. Driving away in her little sports car, Father Gibson warmly stood at the door waving goodbye. Kirsten thought that it was a fascinating combination of religion in one family, but perhaps religion is like a football team. We just all barrack for different teams but with the same goal. It's incredible, though, the number of arguments, wars, and fights over who the best team is.

A few days later, Kirsten sat at her work desk in the Police Station doing the paperwork she'd neglected over the last few days. Never one to be behind or inefficient in any of her delegated tasks, she'd decided to stay back and clear the lot up. The television was on, it had been a quiet day all around, most people had their eyes glued to the TV for the Bath Race, many Australians prayed for Mike, whatever his name was to win, he is such a great iconic rider. However, sadly he blew a front tire, almost winning the race.

As Tommy and Paul bade Kirsten farewell and left for the day, Paul looked back, he came back in, "Look Kirsten, we're off to watch the Basketball at the glasshouse. Would you like to come? It might be good for you," his speech emanated a caring tone. "Thanks, Paul, but I'm focusing on this work, perhaps another night, I've got a heap to do here. We'll catch up soon, mate." He felt hopeful, in a foolish fashion, but disappointed it wasn't now.

As the guys left, the door opened. Father Gibson majestically entered with a vibrantly warm, charismatic smile to boot. "Hello my dear, how would you be today," with a twang of Irish that came up in his speech now and then. Kirsten felt comfortable with this Priest. He had that warm fatherly feel about him. She thought he could be trusted. He explained to her that he'd come seeking information regarding the teen, the adopted child they'd previously spoken about. Kirsten welcomed him in, showing him to her desk, directing him to be seated, venturing off to make him a coffee as he sat patiently observing the present surroundings of the clinically clean Police Station. Kirsten introduced him to the few co-workers that were left in the Police office. The Sarge emerged into the room from his small office, introducing himself. He shook Father Gibson's hand, making his acquaintance, then subtly disappearing just as quickly into another room.

Kirsten set to work on the computers, coming up with ideas and investigating them, looking back into old records that may have given her some clues. Father Gibson got out the yellow pages he carried, following up leads Kirsten gave him, writing down various names and addresses that she recommended or which may provide further leads and information. Hours passed as they both diligently enjoyed working away together. There was this special bond occurring between them, a nice comradeship thing. Eventually drawing to a conclusion that the Juvenile Institution may be the first lead, Kirsten wrote down the women in charge, phone number, and address. There were a few other options. Feeling drawn toward the Juvenile Institution in Preston. His gut feeling told him that was the way to go. They wrapped up their diminutive investigation. He humbly thanked Kirsten with gratefulness and left. "Goodnight, Father." "Goodnight, my child. I'll pray for you tonight." "Man, I need that, although I think God's lost my address," she laughed to herself quietly. "Well, you can thank God you still have a sense of humor, dear," he left smiling. Kirsten looked at the rest of the work on the desk. It was 9.00 p.m. She spent another hour sorting out quite a bit of bookwork, realizing then, there wasn't as much now as she thought.

Tommy arrived early for his night shift. "You still here, Kirsten?" "Yeah, big day in the office," replied Kirsten. "Ya jokin' probably it'll be a quiet night, it'll be hard to stay awake, got any typing for me to do? My book work is all up to date." "Really," replied Kirsten eagerly, "I've got these." "Good, I owe ya 20 favors. It'll be finished by the morning." "Great," she said. Happily packing up, quickly skipping out before he could change his mind. Thinking to herself, *see, one good turn deserves another.* Life wasn't all that bad. Kirsten felt a lot better in herself. It was terrific, and she hoped it was not temporary.

Eight

⊙∞

The Australian sun had just risen as Father Gibson completed his early morning service then set about bidding farewell to his loyal early morning churchgoers. Cleaning down the tabernacle, a voice spoke in his head amidst the angelically peaceful surroundings of the high Church walls. Completing his chores rapidly and precisely, acting spontaneously on his thoughts. He disrobed, quickly dressing in smart priestly attire, then locking up the church doors, hurrying in pursuit of his quest, patiently driving to the address written on the Police calling card. Pulling over, parking directly out front of the enormous Historical building, he felt the Juvenile Institution building looked more like Fort Knox than a comfortable household environment.

Ringing the doorbell set in the cast-iron gate, then gently shaking the gate curiously, in the hope it would open, but alas no, definitely tight security on these gates, he muttered to himself. A deep, golem masculine voice emanated from the gold state-of-the-art tech speaker embedded in the high concrete wall. "State your Security Number," spoke the voice. Surprised, Father Gibson looked around regarding his surroundings, leaning into the speaker to talk, smiling, moving his index finger. He pressed down the button, stating, "I don't have one, sir." A stern voice replied, "State your business." Father Gibson laughed warmly, feeling as though he was talking to a futuristic robot.

As he began to speak, he suddenly observed a tiny camera set in the concrete archway, situated above the cast-iron gates, momentarily admiring such innovative ultramodern technology for the '90s. Father Gibson responded, "I want to speak with a lady by the name of Marion." The golem voice, insisting, "Did you have an appointment?" "No, sir, but if you would be kind enough to let me in, I can explain the situation." Quite dominantly, the voice stated, "No, make an appointment." Father Gibson thought the whole situation to be quite funny. Moving away from the speaker, returning to his car, dialing Marion's phone number on his mobile phone. "Good afternoon, Ms. I would like to make an appointment with you. The Police have given me your office number." Marion listening on the other end of the phone line, resentfully remained in her cold, aloof stance, listening to what she judged as a pathetic cause, stating bluntly she would not see him for another hour. "O.K., that would surely be great, ma'am." Switching off the phone, pulling out his bible from under the seat, picking out various psalms that might help him out with the upcoming foreboding meeting. Father Gibson hadn't dealt with people of this caliber for a long time. For him, it was a very different experience. He prayed the good Lord would bless him with a beneficial outcome on meeting with this woman. Father Gibson checked the time. For some reason, he suddenly began to feel very tired. Father

Gibson perspired slightly from a strange, slight nervous anxiety emanating from his gut. This was most unusual for him. He was always such a happy-go-lucky chap, wondering now if he should drive off and let go of this teenager inquiry quest. Goosebumps rose on his forearms, perhaps, that being a confirmation that he would receive an answer to his prayer after.

The time had come. The hour had dissolved quickly. Moving out of the car, locking it up, taking a deep breath, this time he felt it necessary to try a more serious approach. Ringing the buzzer, he looked straight at the camera, waiting in anticipation. A nervous flutter rose from his being. Surprisingly, the voice had now changed to a husky womanly type. His eyebrows twigged, smiling to himself, suddenly realizing that he had been a victim of his fears which had risen to play a trick with his mind. Thanking God, he had now seen the bigger picture. Pressing the button, then speaking into it, "Father Gibson here to see Marion, I have an appointment."

The large cast-iron gates automatically, dramatically swung open. Stepping in through the gate's archway, then up along the cobbled steps toward the front entrance, two humongous Guards stood and kept watch. Observing to his left, three young youths working in the garden donned in overalls, Akubra hats concealing their heads, bright-colored sunblock covering their noses, protecting them from the bite of the Australian hot sun. The garden was a magnificent array of Australian Bush Flowers and beautifully manicured roses incredibly well maintained. Finally reaching the front door, the two Guards, in perfect synchronicity, opened the colossal front designer steel doors. Father Gibson entered the foyer. Before him, a couple of young girls knelt scrubbing the floors, one looking at him with profound curiosity, speaking not a word, his eyes sent compassion as he bade them a warm 'G'day to you.' One girl stared at the cross which hung from his neck, sending a venomous glare which, for some reason, slightly overwhelmed him. He felt momentarily a little dizzy in the head. He turned suddenly on hearing a husky woman's voice. Vicki stood before him a very sexy young woman, demanding sharply for him to follow her, setting a quick, aggressive pace in and out of corridors, up a broad flight of stairs, passing Guards and high-tech security cameras all the way. Father Gibson thought it was a bit over the top for rehabbing youths, but some suffered from significant drug addiction. Perhaps it was a necessary means. He was grateful for his own good health. Otherwise, he may not have made it to the top of the staircase. It was indeed a mean physical task to perform to get to the top. Entering the masculine, sophisticated office, Marion, calm and sophisticated, stood to greet him in a glacial manner, emanating a hatred of what he represented. She couldn't help but notice his irresistible good looks and fabulous physique, unusual, she thought for a Priest, nothing that she had anticipated. Marion's cold exterior remained solid. Very conservative lust and perversity rose from her loins with a primal urge to want to ruthlessly bonk him on the desktop. Instantly disciplining her wayward thoughts. Focused on his conversation listening to his story concerning the teen in question as Father Gibson sought any information that may lead to finding the whereabouts of the adopted young boy, who by now would have become a teenager if still alive. Marion lapsed from her complex facade momentarily.

Sitting down behind the desk, turning on her laptop computer, checking for the surname he had given her on the scrap piece of paper, but to no avail was there any match given her very brief search through the records. She did provide him with a lead that, perhaps if followed up, may provide some additional answers. Now in her mind, he owed her. She would use him. In some way, she would evilly strategize what that would be. Father Gibson felt an urgency to leave but did so graciously, grateful for the tiny lead information given. He felt strangely uncomfortable and still slightly perspiring nervously. He desperately had to go to the toilet, Marion trying to stall him, picking up telepathically from his aura sphere his urgency to urinate, inwardly riant with herself. Father Gibson, then unable to retain himself any longer, had to diplomatically inquire about the whereabouts of the ablution block. Marion had already secured all security. She didn't feel he was suspicious of anything or that he would be snooping around. She escorted him to the stairs, giving him specific directions to the men's bathroom. His pace quickened. On his quest, he was indeed a little embarrassed.

On the other hand, Marion locked the office door, moved to the wall, pressed in a pin code. The wall opened to reveal a sterile clean room with many screens that viewed all parts of the building. Standing in front of the control panel, she flicked a switch showing a close-up shot of Father Gibson standing in front of the urinal unzipping his fly in haste. She viewed his anatomy, savoring her thoughts for the future. Excited, she felt a throb in her groin as she reached down and felt her groin, knowing he was unaware of being observed.

Suddenly, she was distracted by the phone ringing, it was

her boyfriend, she discontentedly shifted focus back to business, collecting herself returning to the office desk. However, after such extraordinary relief, Father Gibson turned quickly to vacate the toilets only to stumble over the mop being pushed by a very handsome surfie blond teenage boy, who was absorbed in deep thought, unaware of the Priest being in the same room. Suddenly realizing what he had done accidentally with the mop to Father Gibson's shoes, Daniel, startled, apologized profusely. Daniel was really on edge due to living in this facility. It had started to get to him. Daniel had always prided himself in being such a calm, easy-going sort of a dude, and now realized living in this energy didn't suit him, all kinds of things were happening in his head, the most bizarre head trips that didn't feel all that good. Daniel was coming undone. He had to get out, but how? Feeling at points like a caged lion, unable to breathe, it was suffocating. All the rules and dominant stuff didn't suit his laid-back style. His friends had lost themselves in panic, grasping at new concepts driven by their fears, so there hadn't been much of a supportive emotional bond with his comrades of late. As he stood back to look at the Priest, Daniel felt he knew him from somewhere but couldn't place him. Checking the Security Cameras instantly in case someone had noted the mishap. Warmly, Father Gibson greeted the young lad with a friendly "G'day"; suddenly, Daniel turned a paler shade of grey, freezing in his tracks, unable to move. Overwhelmed by a visual apparition floating in the air, momentarily thinking he was tripping. Daniel's body tingled with a strange sensation due to such a familiar presence, although the intensity overpowering, behind to the Priest's right, appeared an ethereal vision of Ester (his once loving foster Mother). She held out her hand, Daniel's mouth dropped. She spoke into his mind. Only he could hear her. "Father can help you. It's safe." The white light disappeared instantaneously into the air as quickly as it had arrived. Father Gibson was confused. Daniel wondered if this was an illusionary game, instigated by the cult, affecting him immensely, feeling weak, mistrusting, and misplaced, Daniel reeling back amidst his fear now collected himself. For quite some time now, he had kept a small piece of paper folded delicately in an obscure hiding place entwined in his clothing with the words, Help Satanic Cult Hostage, inscribed upon it, should by chance an occasion for help to escape to the outside world arise. Panic arising within, indecisive as to how safe he was to make the break and hand over the note to the Priest, suddenly the Priest stated, "I know who you are, Ester Talbot was your foster Mother wasn't she? I thought you looked, familiar lad. Well, I'll be. How did you end up in here, son?" "Ester and I were friends for years," stated Father Gibson. Daniel knew he had to make a move. It was now or never. checking the cameras and maneuvering the Priest slightly to the right out of the sight of the visual camera range, Daniel stated, "Father, you've dropped something." Bending down swiftly, passing a small piece of paper to the Priest. He winked at the Priest, who didn't even question Daniel's motive, feeling intuitively the need to play along, 'Yeah mate, I recognize ya now. Good to see you. I have to continue with my chores sir, Perhaps we'll speak another time." Daniel physically turned his back on the Priest to hide his fear of being discovered by the Guards, who controlled the cameras. The Priest felt a tad rejected and then decided to leave the premises. He left the ablution block, walking toward the Guards, whose job was to open the very secured large front steel doors. The place had so much protection it was almost airtight, Father Gibson thought to himself. Standing still, the alarm went off, the door opened, and he praised the Lord as the Australian sun beamed through the opening onto his face, feeling glad to be out of such a restrained establishment, walking toward the front gates which opened automatically for him to leave. As he turned to look behind, the overlarge gates banged closed suddenly, almost in his face, it was as though he felt the presence of someone watching him, or near him, perhaps he thought to himself. It was paranoia from the high-tech security cameras placed everywhere. Father Gibson got into his car and drove down the road. It was a relatively warm day. The stoplight turned red, on braking, he suddenly broke out into a sweat. He pulled out his handkerchief from his pocket, the small piece of screwed-up paper jumped onto his lap. Still driving, he picked it up. Holding the steering wheel with one hand, he unraveled the note, stunned by the message, "Holy Christ," he said aloud, hitting the brakes, instantly in shock, the car behind him screeched its wheels, and a young mad lad yelled a heap of Aussie slang at him as he angrily overtook the Priest's car. Father Gibson quickly pulled the car over into the gutter. Thank God he was out of sight from the building he'd just left. He blessed himself from blaspheming. The written scribbled words on the crumpled small piece of paper, "Help," rung out to him, "satanic cult hostage," it didn't add up. Father Gibson breathed in profoundly, pondering the conception of some teenage prank, but his holy knowing didn't believe it was a farce. After all, he had experienced some bizarre sensations at that Juvenile Institutional building. The dilemma set in, what was he going to do? This was indeed an incredible responsibility, and how does one explain that to the average everyday Social Services.

Nine

Kirsten sat in a blank state of existence at her desk in the Police office, staring at the computer screen, viewing a long list of convictions committed by various drug offenders. It was a wild stab in the dark as far as this case. The guys in the Police Station were all pretty relaxed tonight on the job. The only call out they'd had in the last 4 hours was this adolescent drug OD at the Mall that Kirsten now had to investigate. Kirsten momentarily analyzed the motive and various thought processes connected with these youths in such a drug-related state. Wondering what possessed them to lose all concept of safety and self-respect, just to experiment with such dangerous designer drugs that were rapidly killing young teenagers within Australian Society. It amazed Kirsten their need for such co-dependency on the adrenaline rush to live in such a continued altered negative state of reality. Her thoughts drifting in and out of dimensions, then falling back into present reality occasionally, her focus shifting to memories of Shane, triggering off pangs of misery, identifying the grief of missing him being around the house and in her life. Tonight, she really couldn't be bothered being on some witch hunt to discover and disclose information on solving some suicidal death in the Mall. All she felt at present was her heartbreak.

The front entrance screen door swung open, Father Gibson entered into the reception area, which was a little sparsely furnished entrance. He leaned over the large wooden counter and rang the bell for assistance. Staring at the large glass mirrors in front of him, aware that he was being observed by quite a few Police behind the screen, at least Father Gibson felt safe in a roundabout way. He'd opt to ask for Kirsten. She may be more compassionate to his cause, especially once he showed her the note, she may even think it a rather excessive worry, but at least he'd put to rest his concerns regards this mission. He'd found Daniel's whereabouts.

Paul came in, handing her a photocopy of a tattooed wrist of the dead youth from the Mall. "Have a look at this," he stated. Kirsten reluctantly taking hold of the paper, only glimpsing it slightly. On sighting Father Gibson, she dismissed the photo and placed it on her desk. She moved forward in a more uplifting frame of mind, opened the door to greet Father Gibson, shook his hand, and ushered him in around the counter through the busy large Police office and down toward her desk. Making him welcome with a generous offer of coffee. He sat down, making sure to be comfortable, indulging in brief, lighthearted banter with the other Police discussing the soccer on TV. He felt relieved Kirsten was on duty. She, too, was glad to have a break from the monotony of the job. Father Gibson felt like a breath of fresh air.

As they chatted, sipping their coffee, Father Gibson discreetly produced the evidence of the crumpled note written by Daniel. Explaining his most recent ordeal on how he had obtained such information while at the same time subconsciously seeking Kirsten's reassurance and advice. Kirsten offered at this point, not even a facial expression. Kirsten decisively tapping on a few keys on the computer keyboard, the screen lit up. "What's the boy's surname? Do you know Father?" "Well, I don't think it's been changed since he was a wee lad residin' with Ester, it would still have to be Heally, Ester changed it by deed poll when she adopted him, the saint of a woman she was, and he too, at that point a good little lad. The poor child must have lost the path of the good lord due to life's blows. I must pray for him." "Well, Father," as Kirsten observed the screen, "I think you may need a little more than that. According to his criminal record, it's a bit more than just a short story here." As Father Gibson leaned over to sneak a peek, "Lordy, Lordy, it's almost a history book. I'll be having the Congregation praying for weeks. I best be ringing my brother's Buddhist monks. They spend hours squatting doing healing chants for troubled souls, you know." I think Daniel will be needin' as many of those as he can get," as he looked at Kirsten with a handsomely cheeky grin. "It appears to me Father Gibson, on deeper review, that most of the time he hasn't been the instigator, he just seemed to be in the wrong place at the wrong time, more of a bystander even, than an accessory to the fact. Hmmm...

Interesting," sighed Kirsten. "It would appear to me then, if you don't mind my opinion Kirsten, that he's still in the wrong place at the wrong time. Do you think he could have been foolin' with this note?" Father Gibson's eyes awash with concerned curiosity. After a momentary silence, Kirsten observed the screen. She regarded Father Gibson and then the note. Breaking her silence, staring, consuming almost his soul. "Father Gibson, suddenly I feel we're on some strange, unusual mission." He nodded, agreeing, with anticipated excitement in the resonance of his voice, "God knows, so what would our next step be then, Dear." "Father, number one, I don't want to hurt your feelings here, but you're not legally allowed to be involved, you know," replied Kirsten staunchly. "Well, I must be able to do something," verbally standing his ground. "Yeah, there is. Ring the Buddhist monk for starters, so he can start chanting. We may need all the help we can get, hah." Although Kirsten spoke her words of jest, a chill ran down her spine like a swift laser beam, sending goosebumps rising instantaneously on her forearms. Continuing her conversation with Father Gibson, explaining to him she remembered doing a check on a car recently, associated with the Juvenile Institution, recalling recognizing the teenager in question previously when on an outing to the local cinema with Shane, her ex.

The blonde woman driver of the vehicle had stood out more in Kirsten's mind at the time. Kirsten had left that on hold when the investigation revealed a Government-owned car belonging to the Juvenile Institution. According to various Counsellors, part of the retraining in these Rehab facilities was getting the teenagers back out in the Community, with supervision, learning to budget, living and participating in "normal life," whatever classification that could be and who knows how that compared to the rehab for teens at this Juvenile Institution. Kirsten, deep in thought, leaned back in her chair, feet crossed elevated and outstretched up on the desk, lips pursed, eyes focused on the screen, profoundly contemplating what her next move would be. Father Gibson stared at her, trying to hide his adrenaline rush of excitement. However, he quietly questioned his motives to the Good Lord, wondering if they were triggered only from the darker side of his own alter ego. Consoling himself with the notion that his mission was purely from the good side of the heart, to help rescue Daniel, whose life, according to Father Gibson opinion, had become that of a tortured, tormented young soul. Perhaps triggered by the devastating death of Daniel's beloved Foster mother, Ester, who happened to be also a very dear loyal friend of his own and a long-time devout member of his Catholic Congregation. "Perhaps I could look at going over to the Juvenile Institution and have a little chat to the blonde, just sus' her out a little," commentated Kirsten. It may give me some insight into something." Now entering overhearing her last sentence, Paul inquired, "do you want me to come to?" "No thanks, Paul, I'll be right." She replied. Paul, still checking in, "I'll ring you in a couple of hours to see how you went." He waited for her response. "No worries," she casually replied. "Where's Linda?" "It's her birthday. She'll be down at the Police Club, drinking," jovially replied Paul. "Hmm," sighed Kirsten. Standing up to move. "Well, Father, I'm out of here. Look, if you come up with anything you know where I am, I'll be back later. Here's a card." Proceeding to jot the number down. "I'll just write my mobile number on it," handing it over. "Ring me if you need to and if you hear any other leads." "Well, thank you, my dear. I'm grateful for that. He leaned over the desk to write her name and number on his business card," so he'd remember whose number it was. He bade her farewell. Waved goodbye to all and left the Police Station, walking to his car. He slowed his pace down as he neared his car. Something inside his gut wouldn't rest, just going back to the Church at the moment didn't feel right. He felt something was unfinished. When you get that intuitive vibe, it keeps on nagging at you. He kept visualizing that symbol of the tattoo photocopied on Kirsten's desk belonging to another youth that had died in the Mall. It kept flashing in his head, contemplating. He unlocked his car door, sat down inside, hands clasping the steering wheel. He observed Kirsten getting into the Police Car and driving out of the Police car park into the heavy traffic of Edwards Street. Suddenly, it dawned upon him to follow Kirsten. A rush flowed throughout his very fit body, tingling lively in his blood. Father pulled out quickly into the main road and followed the Police Patrol Car two cars ahead of him. Nearing the corner, he broke into a nervous sweat, wondering if the good lord thought this would be o.k. He raised his eyes to the heavens and blessed himself quickly, then placing both hands on the steering wheel instantly to drive safely. In Father Gibson's mind eye, it seemed forever to reach the point of destination. Concern arose in the pit of his stomach. What if Kirsten arrested him for hindering and intervening in Police matters. Surely, she wouldn't, but she may, given she was so adamant when advising him that he was not to involve himself in Police issues, as it was against the law. Father Gibson felt it his duty to at least see Daniel one more time. This seemed almost the perfect opportunity. Kirsten pulled up on the side of the road, slightly away from the view of security cameras and the large cast-iron gates to the Institution. Sitting in the car, she radioed in to establish her whereabouts to Police communications, then checked her gun and radio, feeling uneasy, on edge, and very ready. She was alone due to staff cut issues, once again an outcome of the cutbacks. Writing down on the report sheet the time and her whereabouts. Next minute the Police car door opened, startling her. Instantly collecting herself, to maintain a sanguine facade, it was only Father Gibson. "What are you doing here?" A kayoed Kirsten demanded abruptly. "Now, my dear, I can't be having a blessed child as yourself entering the walls of the unknown without a protector, can I... hmmm?" said with a silver smooth Irish tongue. Kirsten softened slightly but remained intransigent that he was intruding in an area not warranted, that her work was strictly confidential, and certainly didn't involve civilian assistance in this instance.

Father Gibson remaining persistent, "Look, I wouldn't be interfering, I only want to see Daniel for a split second to discretely give him my number, and then my mission will be over if it is the wish of the good Lord." They bantered verbally momentarily. Kirsten gave in. She had no idea why, thinking her reaction most strange and out of character for her. The pair got out of the car, walking toward the austere solid large cold cast-iron gates. Father Gibson suddenly felt a little lightheaded. He reached for Kirsten's arm, who flinched abruptly. Kirsten observed his face turn as white as a ghost. Questioning him with concern in her voice. He replied, "I'm feeling weird in the body like it would be the chill of death walkin' over my grave. Would you 'have experienced that sensation before? This place exudes a negative presence to me, and I don't know why." The color instantly returned to his face. Both stopping short in front of the dreaded security camera. As a Police Officer, Kirsten had the authority to attend these premises whenever it was necessary, so, therefore, there would be no hold-up getting inside the door. A loud, gravel authoritative voice spoke, asking for details. Kirsten diplomatically offering the information required by a Police Officer. They entered in through the sudden opening of the gates.

Father Gibson stuck close by like glue. They ventured toward the huge security steel doors of the Juvenile Institution, which opened in synchronicity, being greeted by two huge Museum Guards and the blonde Vicky. How appropriate, thought, Kirsten, just the woman in question they wanted to speak with, and she was emanating such an arrogant, superior vibe. Interestingly enough, both Father Gibson and Kirsten fleetingly made eye contact, telepathically connecting into the same train of thought. Vicky sensed the vibe between them instantaneously being possessed of acute psychic abilities, drawing in the negative energy of her alter ego, balancing the vibration, enabling her persona to then be more subtly camouflaged. "What exactly were you wanting?" Vicky now asking in a staunch gravel tone. Kirsten proceeded to speak. Right at that precise moment, three of the teenage boys walked toward them, almost in militant fashion, all in step, bearing ashen looks on their faces. When within one meter, Father Gibson moved with tenacity, recognizing Daniel, grabbing his hand as quickly as an arrow, he slipped a business card into the boy's hand so fast it was almost impossible for the human eye to have noticed,

Kirsten had dropped her Police calling card on the ground

simultaneously, bending immediately to retrieve it. All eyes were on Kirsten, Vicki's included. Then while shifting her focus, Vicki suddenly realized Father Gibson's spontaneous rush, losing control momentarily arm rigidly outstretched, pointing to Father Gibson instructing him he had no permission to move about freely within the Juvenile Institution. There was no physical contact to be made with any of the Juvenile teenagers residing within the Institution's walls. Kirsten still crouched to the ground, momentarily frozen in the spot, looking up at Vicki's arm vacillating over her, revealing a strange tattoo on Vicki's wrist. Suddenly Kirsten's thoughts came into perspective. Her analytical detective mind switched into overdrive. Vicky quickly modified her control issue as Father Gibson profusely apologized, explaining he wasn't trying to cause any conflict. He was just happy to see the teenage boy, as he knew who Daniel was.

Vicky snapped loudly that to contact anyone in there, one would have to go through the correct procedure and be authorized to do so by Marion, the woman in charge. Kirsten spoke in a calm, controlled authoritarian manner to match Vicki's stance. "Well then, I would like to meet with her now." Vicky stared her straight in the eye, finding Kirsten rather sexually attractive. Her exterior physical shell appeared fit and very in shape. Vicky knew the woman had guts, feeling the need to back off with her own power trip. Now informing them that Marion was presently out of Melbourne attending a conference and returning in a few days. Offering to submit the Card to Marion on her return. Directly ushering Father Gibson and Kirsten out of the building. Moving swiftly in dead silence to the large cast-iron gates, which flew back ferociously locking, aided by the gust of fierce, strong cold wind, almost bowling both of them over, sending goosebumps eerily rippling over their skin. In control of the situation, Kirsten moved quickly and effectively to the car, unlocking the door, ensuring both were safe inside the vehicle, out of range of cameras and voice detectors.

Once safely inside the car, Father Gibson reacted with the words "Holy Jesus," instantly raising his eyes to the roof, blessing himself, clasping his hands in prayer for a split second, then bowing. Kirsten breathed deep and remained calm, then gently sighed. Looking at him, he was afraid and trying to recuperate quickly from the heart palpitations caused by his weird ordeal. "Father Gibson, what on Earth were you trying to achieve? You're supposed to converse with me. If you're going to make moves like that on the job, at least we need to have some sort of plan of attack that could create a successful outcome, instead of it turning out to be a botch-up," Attempting to counteract her statement. "On the contrary, my dear, it was a wonderful decoy, unbeknown to anyone noticing. Daniel now has my contact number."

Kirsten looked at him curiously, "With a wee wink of an eye, I slipped him my card, not even you noticed." He stated with glee. Exasperated, "Father, Father, Father," Cool and calm Kirsten shook her head with a slight smile. Father Gibson now looked pleased as punch with his win, "one more thing," did you not notice the tattoo on the blonde bombshell as she raised her arm to me? I've seen that symbol somewhere before. It's been skipping through my head. Vicky was like a wild banshee." Kirsten butted in, " I just kept seeing that tattoo for the last hour through this hair-raising ordeal

Father," Kirsten replied, "May I remind you that this is not a movie we're participating in here. It's real Australian Police life. It could be dangerous, not to mention extremely detrimental to your health. Now, do you have your mobile?" "Yes," he replied, "Right in my hot little blessed hand," Kirsten ordered him to ring the Presbytery, notifying the altar boys to wait for him inside the front door with the lights on. She would follow him home to ensure his safety, instructing him to take them back route into the Church grounds in case someone was following.

As night fell quickly, he drove home. Father Gibson was in a merry little mood. Feeling relatively chuffed with his significant achievement, as he swiftly drove his vehicle merrily through the back gates of the Catholic Church, slowing down instantly. Boy, he had to get on to this tomorrow. Father Gibson hadn't realized how dark it was out there. It was eerie. He suddenly felt unsafe. The graveled road made driving difficult. He hit the high beams, revealing some of the larger gravestones. All of a sudden, he hit the brakes in shock. Before him, larger than life, the face of a demon floated in the air outside his window screen. Terror rattled through his loins, a distorted demonic voice spoke loudly to him, "I will get you," in a long drawn out drawl tone. In an instant, the apparition vanished. Father Gibson's skin crawled by the impact of the dark entity, shaking his head doubting his vision. Cold unnerving energy permeated his entire being. Kirsten hit the brakes of the Police Patrol Car, nearly running into his now stationary vehicle. She rang his mobile. The loudness in the stillness of the dark echoed, causing him to jump in fright, bringing him back into this present dimension.

"What the hell are you doing?" she questioned him. He stuttered fearfully, "Da da did you see that?" "See what?" She snapped. "Nothing, I must be overtired. My imagination must be running away with me." "Perhaps," Kirsten replied, "Like you're ever-exciting quest to unravel mysteries while on so-called dramatic missions." "Yeah," shaking his head, he couldn't define reality from where he was presently sitting. Pulling up in his car, he ran inside quickly, warmly met by the altar boys. Kirsten drove up behind him, then alongside his vehicle, beeped the horn, checking his safe arrival as she could see he was now in the house. Leaving the grounds, returning directly to the Police Station, seeking more information regarding the mysterious tattoo and the blonde bombshell Vicky.

Father turned on all the lights of the Presbytery, lit all the blessed candles in the establishment, ordered everyone in the household to sleep in the main living room. The four members of the house were asked to participate in solid prayer for half an hour. They all anointed themselves with holy water from Lourdes. Father Gibson burnt sage sticks to protect the house, and then bibles were placed in all four corners of the room they were sleeping in. An unusual ritual induced by fear.

No one questioned his motive, although the younger altar boy Heath thought it rather odd. Eventually, Father Gibson fell into a disturbing restless sleep, reaching only minimal depths of rem, on guard with emotion. Anticipating war should the need arise for him to jump up physically to attack some avenger trying to invade their blessed holy sanctuary. Tomorrow he would speak to Kirsten and explain this unusual ordeal. Perhaps she may have experienced the same incident at some stage.

Ten

Now back at Police Headquarters, Kirsten sat upright in her office chair, typing as she concentrated on the computer, checking for clues through security codes, names, Government Offices, addresses that may give further information on Vicky. Who was this woman? Then like domino's simultaneously falling, the answers unraveled before Kirsten's eyes on the screen. "Ah-ha, bingo!" Speaking aloud to herself, although the ever-present interested Paul being within earshot, ever so curious, just had to ask, "What have ya got?" "Well, well, look at this!" Kirsten replied, beaming with the look of achievement. "Seems like the blonde bombshell Vicky is not only the queen of being a thug but has been done for two counts of prostitution. One fraud charge, and suspect for an extortion investigation and charged for aiding and abetting in a drug scam. This poses the question given these facts. How did she obtain a position in her present place of employment?" Kirsten sat intrigued. "Let's have a look," Paul warmly leans over Kirsten, viewing the screen, utilizing the opportunity to move in very close to Kirsten physically. Curiously, Paul posed the question, "who'd wanna bonk that bag of bones? Check out the tats." Kirsten squinted, zooming in to enlarge the visual of the Tattoo. It appeared identical to the photocopy Paul placed on her desk two days ago. Perplexed, Kirsten concentrated on the screen. What did that Tattoo signify, though? It wasn't just you're run of mill tattoo. It bears unusual lettering that didn't add up to a word as such. There was a type of Phoenix Fire Bird set within a circle. Then bold black lettering on the inside of the circle, the word, 'Kernunous' was inscribed, a phrase meaning, "who is so great?" Paul studied it for a split second, then responded, "who knows, mate!" Kirsten is serious, although quietly riant inwardly at his poor attempt to be a comedian. Suddenly now aware of his almost embrace around her, she subtly distanced herself away from him by rolling a further few inches away on her swivel chair out of his reach, appearing as if to move away to reach for the A4 photocopy of the symbolic Tattoo. At that precise moment, Shane arrived in view, abruptly stopping in his tracks. His manly muscle-bound body stood rigid, suddenly breaking into a sweat on his observation of Kirsten and Paul as his jealousy issue rose. In a sarcastically dry tone, Shane spat out the words, "Having fun?" Directing a sharp, bitter resonance, triggered instinctively by pure male territorial enviousness. Even though he knew that he and Kirsten were no longer an item, his disrespectful dialogue was unwarranted, especially in the workplace. "Don't mind him," quipped Paul, in quick retaliation, "it's just the juice talking." Shane threw him an evil glare. Shane had to leave the room swiftly, as he knew his steroid addiction would make him lose control. Through the glass window of the closed door, Kirsten stood pensive from a distance observing Shane, who had moved far away to another building area. In a rage, he aggressively punched the brick wall in the corridor of the other building. Her face was forlorn as her eyes teared for a second and her heart grew heavy, then as she took a deep breath, in the blink of an eye, her optimistic logic suddenly kicked in, overriding the deep pain of the moment. Kirsten recognized that she was beginning to heal from the ending of their relationship, although a slower process than she wanted, progress was apparent. The horrendous pain of her broken heart was slowly beginning to heal. From a practical point of view anyway, what good to her was someone who had turned into the nightmare from hell, driven by pure vanity and destructive impulsive aggressive behavior triggered by steroids and substance abuse. The relationship, no doubt, from his irrational reactions, would only result in a harmful or dangerous outcome. Shane may momentarily revel in a fleeting limelight moment of fame on stage, winning one very highly competitive competition. Inevitably, he may end up making himself physically and dangerously ill. In most aspects of his persona, Shane's daily behavioral patterns were out of control and highly questionable. This would only lead to his success amounting to nothing. It was Kirsten who could see the writing on the wall, and she knew at the end of the day, she had given him 150%. He had to resolve his own issues with no point in rescuing someone who doesn't want to help himself. Although pangs of deep love for him were still etched in her heart, and at times her heart ached for him. She had to let those feelings go and keep moving forward in her life. She refused to tolerate abuse from a man.

As Kirsten climbed into her soft, warm bed that night,

aware Shane's sarcasm had cut her deep emotionally, she snuggled into the feather-down pillow, a hurtful little tear rolled down from her big beautiful brown eyes. Time, time would help her heal, she told herself. Time, it's supposed to heal all. As the clock ticked loudly away in the dark of the night. Unable to sleep. The digital clock whose luminous numbers stood out starkly in the darkness read 10.00 pm and continued to click on.

The phone ringing suddenly echoed loudly in the stillness of the night, automatically answered by her machine, the volume on high. Kirsten stirred from her light slumber. She couldn't be bothered answering it. "Kirsten, are you home? It's Shane." His tone was somber. Overwhelmed with surprise, she sat bolt up in bed listening. A second silence, and then he hung up. Kirsten rolled over in her bed, not knowing what to think, her eyes staring at the ceiling for a time. She shook her head in frustration. Then tossing and turning for a while, she finally fell into a deep sleep. Waking early, feeling sluggish, participating in her usual run around Edwards Lake. Enjoying the sun coming up over the gum trees, weeping willows, hearing the ducks quacking, and getting some fresh air after a rough, emotionally charged night, putting a few miles in her legs would indeed ground and center her. Kirsten continued running in a meditative state, still feeling groggy and her psyche still marooned in the dimensions of the astral dreaming planes.

Deciding to return home for a fix of caffeine, her favorite coffee, hoping that may give her that morning lift that was required. A lot of ground had to be covered today. The objective is to solve the riddle of the Tattoo. It may give a definite lead, intricate piece of artwork that it was, a symbol of type, representing something. Although an obvious clue, especially now showing up on other kids that had OD in the mall lately. All of them bearing the same mysterious Tattoo on the inner forearm. What was its significance?

Showered and dressed in casual attire, leaning back in her home office chair, sipping a second cup of coffee that had repurchased her into focus, concentrating on the photocopy of the Tattoo. Staring at it, it appeared to be a circular symbol with some type of phoenix firebird inserted in it. Perhaps it would give her another clue to the puzzle to solve the case. Startled by a sudden break in her surrounding silence, a familiar voice hailed, "Good mornin' to ya' lass. Would ya' be wantin' to share a cuppa' with a friend at this wee hour of the morning..," as a tap on the screen of her open-door revealed Father Gibson's warm Irish presence.

Kirsten glanced toward the door. She shook her head, smiling to herself. "Good morning to you Father, it appears that I can't get rid of you." "Now why would ya' be wantin' to do that when I've been so helpful," replied with a grin, as she sat at her home office desk, still observing the symbol, waiting for an opinion to emerge from his lips as he quietly looked at Kirsten. "Any ideas?" he questioned.

"I rang a psychic colleague last night that the Sarge uses at times to help solve different cases. Judy does Astrology, Tarot, and Healing. She is an Astrologer and Psychic. Judy suggested I try the New Age Shop in Eltham. I may discover some books or something that may lead to helpful information regards the Tattoo. The other alternative is a library, which could be a long-drawn-out process of searching through many books.

I need instant results now to prevent any further deaths of this nature." Kirsten bore a look of compassion as she regards Father Gibson. "Well, make haste, my girl, we best be leavin'."

Resisting, Kirsten stated, "Father Gibson, this is a police matter." "Shh, shh my girl, it's your day off, is it not? It's a casual visit where I'll be takin' ya to visit a friend of mine." Kirsten questioning his chatter as he explained the Clairvoyant at the New Age Bookshop was a friend of his and came to his church regularly. According to the woman herself, whose name was Kathryn, she was of the Christ-like energy who prayed religiously to the likes of Mother Mary and the good Saint Mary MacKillop. Kirsten listened, rolling her eyes to the ceiling, wondering now what the day would bring. Kirsten then decided to go quickly to eradicate this as an option.

"Let's go then, Father Gibson," swiftly grabbed her keys and handbag. "Before we leave Kirsten," halting her to attention, "Did you have any strange experiences when going through the cemetery last night?" Kirsten's reaction sharp, "yes?" He then breathed a sigh of relief. Ready to plunge into the conversation, Kirsten cut in, "it's probably the first time I ever felt like pummelling a Catholic Priest for thrusting on the brakes of his car in a darkened area when I was driving so close to the back end of this car." Apologetically he snapped back, "Oh God, forgive me, dear." Kirsten replied, "I was thinking more along the lines of Jesus Christ." Father Gibson raised a questioning eyebrow, "Would ya' have been praying or blaspheming, is the question?" "A bit of both, I think, Father Gibson." Politely quipped Kirsten as she locks the back door, and the pair left her house. Father Gibson realized that they had not shared the same visual experience, wondering how to broach the subject with Kirsten. Perhaps something would reveal itself in the New Age Shop they were about to attend. He went silent.

Although, feeling it slightly controversial to his religion entering such a shop, he felt comfortable knowing Kathryn to be a good soul, gentle and kind, not of a dark nature, not demonic or barbaric at any cost. Questions rose within him about his religion, his motive in this situation. Where he was in his mind. Last night had been burdensome, long, and plagued with intense, overwhelming fear. His mental anguish almost sent him over the edge, analyzing the analysis. He felt fragile today. Deep in his inner knowing, a strong gut feeling told him to be careful. There was a significant risk and red flags eminent with this current situation. Knowing darkness lay in the journey ahead. Not having felt such physical anxiety for a very long time as that of last night. He and Kirsten must discuss this matter today at some point. It was epochal.

Entering the New Age Shop, walking through the crystal mystical beaded curtains that sent colored rays of dancing light around the room, igniting the large crystals situated on the bookshop's shelves, creating a luminous wonderland effect. With big beautiful crystal jewelry, colored salt lamps, books, the engaging aroma of Nag Char Incense, and angelic ambient music enveloping anyone who entered such an atmosphere. Kathryn emerged from behind the counter dressed in Kirsten's Police description as hippie fashion, bearing a divine presence that emanated such peace and serenity. Kirsten felt a similar likeness to that of a nun who had once been her teacher. How odd, not knowing what to expect, having very little to do with any type of mystic healer before.

Without hesitation, Kathryn embraced Father Gibson with a huge warm hug, exchanging kind words and greetings. Kirsten remained professionally diplomatic, introducing herself as Constable, producing her badge as proof that it was more than a friendly visit. Father Gibson set about speaking. Kirsten intercepted, immediately controlling the conversation.

Father Gibson's chatting faded subtly into the background as Kathryn focused solely on Kirsten, giving her undivided attention. Touching Kirsten gently on the forearm, softly guiding Kirsten in to enter a smaller room, where they could speak in privacy. Father Gibson took up a seat in front of the large bookcase, collecting a couple of books within reach to start his search for anything resembling the likeness of the symbolic Tattoo in question.

Meanwhile, Kirsten felt swept up in a gently hypnotic wave of calmness. Moving graciously along with her like a leaf in the wind at the beckoning of this heavenly-like woman.

Kathryn gently directed Kirsten to sit in the antique spindle back chair. Kirsten sat down, placing her hands on the deep red velvet tablecloth of the exquisite old table. Kirsten refused to be mesmerized by the experience, although aware of the unusual subtle dizzy sensations she was experiencing. Kathryn reassured Kirsten that it may have only been the crystals having a healing effect on her, "they do work in that capacity, you know, they're natures healing gift to the world. Now you have something to show me?"

Kirsten, assertively replying, "did he tell you?" Kathryn laughed. "No, no, Dear. I'm tapping into your psychic scalars." "What's that?" inquired Kirsten. "Everyone has them," replied Kathryn, "they lay in the back of your head. There are three points situated around the pituitary gland. Most people don't know how to control them or how to use them. You can open them up like an antenna, they act as transmitters, and they usually receive high-frequency vibrations from various Multi-dimensional life force energies in different worlds. It assists us in picking up telepathic messages from one person to another or other life forces in the spirit world. The three antennae are for clairvoyance, cardio audience, and telekinesis. The art is in developing these gifts, my Dear." Kirsten felt that it sounded like a science report, although quite fascinated and enthralled by such an intellectual concept as she put forth the piece of paper on the sacred table. "Hmm, hmm, not unsolvable in the least," spoke Kathryn, gazing at the symbol. "Are you aware of its representation?" Kirsten is curious, "I have no idea," replied Kirsten, shaking her head, "but it's haunting me," with a tone half-joking. "Here, I want you to place this holy water on your fingertips and bless your forehead. Repeat after me, Kirsten," 'I call upon my higher self to constantly protect me and keep the Angels and Archangel Michael guiding and protecting me in Christ-like energy to keep me safe in all aspects of my being always." Kirsten felt slightly dizzy when she repeated what sounded like some type of prayer, consoling herself that it felt safe to repeat. After all, what would it hurt?

Kathryn moved her hand to the right, reaching for a pack of cards covered by a purple silk scarf, passing her hand over them clockwise three times. Shuffle them, close your eyes, breathe deeply through your nose. Ask a question in your head. Kathryn, looking impishly at Kirsten, "one question at a time, let's not be too hasty." Kirsten laughed. "Before we move further forward, there will be a reconciliation with your loved one. His soul has a bit of a journey. He has lessons to learn before you reunite. He will come back, but partly a changed man, for the better. You have many admirers that will pursue you, especially those who are close in your working environment. You don't believe a word I'm saying. You are extremely negative regards this reading. You will be happy again in your relationship, don't worry, the spirits are saying". Kirsten rigidly stopped shuffling. "Now they warn me you are in danger, near danger, around danger, in a dangerous job. Of course, spirit," as Kathryn speaks into the air, "this is, after all, a Police Person."

Kathryn spoke fiercely, looking into the air. Kirsten scanned the room to see if anyone else had entered. Goosebumps rose on her arms and up the nape of her neck. It felt creepy. "'Kerrnunous' represents the horned one, heralded as the powerful God of the Darkness. Pagans of Satanic Wicca n worship him as their God. I follow the God of the light. They are both of powerful energy, the light, and the dark. Our thoughts and deeds produce energy, the way we project that energy depicts whether it be good or bad. Remember, my Dear, where thoughts go, energy flows." Kathryn continues to lay out the cards in a Celtic Cross on the table.

"What you are dealing with regards this symbol is one of a satanic nature. Forewarned is forearmed. Good luck, my Dear. I shall send out absent healing for you this evening to keep you safe in this investigation. Father Gibson will know a lot on this subject."

Kirsten was dumbfounded, overwhelmed by the onslaught

of all-consuming information. Sitting motionless in the chair. Shock riveted through Kirsten's being. Wow, is this for real? Questioning her thoughts. Kathryn responded in a definite tone. "Yes, this is for real."

Once again, telepathically picking up on Kirsten's thought processes. Surprised by Kathryn's comment, Kirsten hastily stood, not knowing why such an urgency had come over her to leave the New Age shop. On his discovery through the bookshelf, Father Gibson had unveiled the symbol in a book titled, Paganism in the times of the Dark Ages and Beyond. Kathryn lovingly offered it to him as a gift, escorting them to the door, wishing them well. Waving goodbye, the two hurriedly vacated the premises. They sat in the car for a moment, Kirsten slightly unnerved, looking rather pale from the ordeal, explaining the conversation that had taken place, unraveling extraordinary information. Kirsten turned to Father Gibson, now stunned and a paler shade of Gray. Sudden anxiety rose from his gut. His biggest fear is now confirmed.

He was terrified, with a great cause to be. He knew more than anybody the destruction a Satanic Group can cause. He'd seen the physical evidence projected right before his very eyes. He'd exorcised possessed souls years gone by, and the last time he did that, he'd vowed and declared never to do it again. Once, he'd gone against the Archbishop's wishes to save a teenage girl from the grips of such a cult, overstepping the laws by not adhering to the standard formal written request of the Archbishop.

Father Gibson justified this fleeting memory, feeling by the time he'd passed through the long process of red tape, it would have been too late, the girl would be dead, her soul abandoned and disturbed, sold to the devil. His nonconformity, plus fast reaction, had saved her life. He felt it necessary to aid her cause. At least then he could sleep easy at night. Even a Priest must take a risk to maintain personal religious equilibrium. Having had such an experience dealing with the demonic dark side of an enormously influential unknown abyss left a penetrating fearful scar etched deep in Father Gibson. Riveting memories of extreme dark energy attacking him in the past flooded back, crowding his headspace, causing grave concern, and now once again, the dark was back to haunt him. He knew he had to save Daniel. Somehow, he would do that in his true heroic fashion.

Kirsten knew she couldn't get out of this situation as she was the cop who had to put a lid on the case. Looking at it optimistically, at least she'd solved the mystery of the symbol within that day. That was one goal completed. One box ticked. "How bad could catching a bunch of witches be?" stated Kirsten. Father Gibson scoffed. "Bad," "No, surely not," said Kirsten. "Mmm, bad," confidently he replied with a solemn nod. Kirsten rang Paul at the station on her mobile to quickly check in on any other information that may have come up and could be relevant, but nothing had shown up.

Kirsten slowly pulled out of the car park, heading back home. She needed another coffee. Kirsten was determined to solve this case quickly as it was dragging out and taking way too long. She felt she needed a holiday.

Eleven

Almost nearing home, Kirsten suddenly pulled over, coming up with the profound idea to go and speak to Judge Bennetton. She'd known him through the job for almost 6 years, having had numerous dealings with him through various Court Cases and Juvenile Aid Panel proceedings. "Father Gibson, do you mind if I call in, it's on the way home, but you'll have to wait for me in the car, OK?" "OK." he passively agreed. "Sure, I won't be holding you up?" asked Kirsten curiously. "No, no, not in the least child, there's one confession on my agenda for later on tonight, that's all." "Now, Father, what would you be confessing to?" she said with a laugh. With a direct unusual serious reply to her, "I'll be severely prayin' that we survive this ordeal." "Oh, OK, you'd best do that," said Kirsten, agreeing with him wholeheartedly.

Pulling up in the long drive of the statuesque historical old courthouse. Kirsten opted for parking out of the back area of the building. Knowing where Judge Bennetton's office was located in the building, having left from the back entrance many a time regards discussions on several cases. Priding herself in knowing the security code to enter, pressing the buttons, the security door opened, exposing a magnificent hallway of unique antique quality, endowed with a stately monstrous elaborate, ornate ceiling. In Kirsten marched assertively, ready to make herself quite at home. About to turn the corner, suddenly viewing the unfamiliar face of a young dark-haired woman, whom Kirsten was not familar with. Kirsten stopped in her tracks, staring into the mirror off the overmantle, feeling a sudden need to backtrack. Maybe the office had been changed around perhaps, she thought to herself. One should retreat swiftly before appearing somewhat overly confident. Turning around to walk away promptly, standing staunchly in the hallway, appeared the Judge. "Hi, Judge Benneton, just who I'm looking for?" He returned a blank stare, appearing slightly confused by Kirsten's presence. "I let myself in. How are you? Have you lost a bit of weight? Have you been training for another marathon? That happened to you last time, remember."

Judge Benneton stood there in silence. Kirsten continued chatting, "are you busy? I just called in for a coffee and a quick chat." Taking privilege, entering his large office, making herself comfortable, plonking herself down in the chesterfield club chair.

Judge Benneton cautiously followed and sat, too enthralled by her beauty, listening to her story. The dark-haired woman entered, carrying silverware full of tea and coffee. Acknowledging the woman's presence. "Thank you, Ramona!" She dipped her head to him submissively in silence and left the room.

"What happened to the faithful Diane?" Kirsten inquired. There was a pregnant pause of silence before he spoke in his strong eloquent, educated tone, "She left in a huge hurry." "That's unusual for Diane," replied Kirsten, dismissing her interest.

Immediately focusing on her mission. Hoping that some information may arise through Judge Bennetton shedding some light on the Juvenile Institution where the teenagers live. Or if he knew about any other events or goings-on which have occurred at the Juvenile Institution. Alas, to Kirsten's disappointment, he offered not a skerrick of information to assist her investigation.

The afternoon sun fading cast shadows that emanated through the high french double doors. Kirsten briefly glancing out of them, observing through the beautiful atrium of ferns, her car in the back car park, then very close to the open window, staring straight in at her, and Judge Benneton, was none other than Father Gibson. Kirsten instantly looked straight at the Judge, dismissing herself almost immediately. She was pissed off with Father Gibson defying her instructions. In the meantime, Father Gibson had swiftly crouched down and scurried back to the car, realizing her wrath, sitting waiting in anticipation, he knew she was angry. Getting into the car, Kirsten slammed the door abruptly, winding up the window in total silence, driving hurriedly out of the gates, then, when safe to do so, pulled over to the side of the road. He knew he'd pushed her buttons, seething she barked, "Don't ever do that to me again, Father Gibson, who the hell do you think you are to be so disrespectful?" she growled, shook her head, unable to speak further at that point. She instantly shut down and remained silent. The silence was deafening to Father Gibson, who had to break it with the statement, "Judge

Benneton looks vaguely familiar to me, but he's not part of my congregation." "I would expect not," replied Kirsten, in short, not wanting to continue any form of communication. As Kirsten drove down the road, they sat in deathly silence.

Recalling her conversation with Judge Bennetton, she knew she hadn't divulged too much police information. Although Father Gibson was becoming a worry, his keenness at times appeared slightly irrational, which could lead to complications and that responsibility falling back onto her, and may even jeopardize her job. Kirsten didn't need the crap. And indeed, didn't need the stress of impulsiveness ruining the investigation. At present, it was excess emotional baggage she couldn't afford.

After Kirsten had left Judge Bennetton's office, he sat deliberating his move, mulling

over their conversation, then pressing the intercom, ordering Romana to collect his large briefcase, cancel his last appointment, switch on the answering machine, and instructing her to drive him over to the Juvenile Institution.

He stared out of the window. The full lunar moon was already appearing in the sky, and so early, it was inspiring. He got out of the passenger seat of the Mercedes, bade Ramona farewell, instructing her that he would call her if he required her services later. He watched the car drive off down the large driveway through the large cast-iron gates and down the prestigious deserted street. Although it was still only late afternoon, the sky grew dark, caused by sizeable heavy grey thunderous clouds. He stood out in front of the iconic historic building porch alone. It looked like a fortress to behold. A strange smirk glided across his face as he wondered what the night would bring. He pressed the bell on the concrete wall, explaining he had an appointment with Marion.

As he walked through toward the entrance, the gates opened, lighting suddenly shot across the Melbourne sky, leaving a chill in the air. Once on the inside, he was instructed to meet her up in the communications camera control room, next to her office at the top of the long flight of impeccably polished wooden jar-rah stairs, which he proceeded to climb.

Tash, amidst her ignorant adolescence, now becomes mesmerized by the dark solid powers that some of these women possessed within the establishment's walls. As if the mind played trickery on one's sight. Captivating her in a visual illusion, constantly observing their games. Testing the force of the strength of their mental agility against one another, almost in some warlike energy competitive quest.

There was preparation today. Tash had decided she wanted to possess that power. She wanted that gift, which would give her that extraordinary power to control other human beings, just by pure telepathic thought. It would mean, so she thought, she could do almost anything or have anything she wanted. Oh, to feel that power. Perhaps she may use it to escape where no one would find her nor wish to pursue her. She would fade into nonexistence. She would look to bewitch Daniel, perhaps.

The anticipated excitement of tonight's initiation for her had escalated over the last three days, having her ego pumped to the max, not knowing what she would experience. She enjoyed the pampering of complete body wax, her beautiful head of hair and eyebrows attended to. They'd given her the symbolic tattoo on the inside of both wrists, the size of a twenty-cent piece. It stung only minimally, as they'd applied some strange herb to delete any pain and to make it heal quickly. Through a projection of energy, they'd somehow accessed Tash's DNA levels to speed up the healing process at a phenomenal rate using some form of energy frequency transference.

"Tash" came a loud distinctive voice into the kitchen. Tash turned swiftly to respond to the voice. Marion entered the kitchen, drawing very close into Tash's proximity. Invading her personal space, stroking Tash's hair, almost in a fleeting sensual tender touch. Marion's voice softened on this occasion, "'Kerrnunous' will love your innocence, it will be spellbinding, it is the beginning of your initiation over some time to obtain strong powers that have lain dormant within your soul for eons. After tonight you become a Mer mail."

Not having an understanding of the actual title. It sounded good to Tash, who never before had felt so important. Her ego grew to voluminous heights, creating an illusion state of grandiose and importance. "You are to finish your duties now, it is exactly 6.00 p.m. You will go to the staff shower block.". Adhering to Marion's dominant orders, she put down the utensils willingly, moving quickly to the elite staff ablution quarters where only staff members usually showered and certain unknown rituals were held.

The smell of aromatics engulfed her nostrils. It was intense and heady. The exquisite overly large spa bath had been run, filled to the brim with luscious, inviting soap suds, perfumed oils, and exotic moisturizer, which she thought was exciting. Then she was given the order to undress. She stepped slowly down naked into the warm, overly large bathtub escorted by two other women, also staff members already initiated into the fold, and had been for quite some time. Although only recently employed at the Institution, they too, their beautiful bodies naked, submerged themselves into the warm, inviting massive aromatic bath. Vicky entered, wearing a thin see-through, black shrouded robe, tied only by a black cord and wearing nothing underneath.

Vicky held three gold chalices meant for each woman. Vicky was radiant, aglow with the forthcoming event. She enjoyed being a participant in this part of the ritual. It suited her to a tee. African drumbeats pulsated throughout the ablution area, adding sound effects to the atmosphere, slowly and sensually invoking the dark primal energy within them all. A massage table stood erect, red fur covering its entire length visible under dimly lit atmos ceiling and candle lights.

Tash and the other two young women frolicked playfully and provocatively. Standing up, occasionally cavorting their naked bodies in front of Vicky, who remained the observer, seated on a tiny throne that had been placed right at the head of the enormous spa bath and was semi-submerged in the warm water of the bubble bath. Enjoying the arousal. The Kundalini energy rose in Vicky's loins. Lustful thoughts deepening as she opened her legs, causing the black sheer sensual silk to slide across her skin, unveiling her partially waxed crotch. Proudly displaying three sleeper earrings pierced through one side of her waxed labia, an extroverted sexual masochistic appendage she enjoyed wearing. Leaning over, handing a chalice of a drug concocted wine to the unsuspecting Tash, who gleefully launched into woofing down the drink.

Vicky came very close to Tash's face, preventing Tash from sculling the mixture with such haste. "Slowly, slowly, my pet, drink slowly of the divine wine." Vicky sensually slid her finger over Tash's thick luscious pouting lips. Collecting remnants of red wine that dribbled down her chin, then Vicky licked the concoction from her finger in a robust sexual fashion, getting high from the ecstasy buzz of the drug. Vicky tantalizingly licking Tash's lips, Tash's head became light, overcome by sexual uninhibited actions. Her body is now being aroused by the two women caressing and embracing her. Vicky moved in the warm water like a slow serpent maneuvering itself toward Tash's body. Vicky slid into a sitting position on the inbuilt small bench seat in the spa, parting her legs on either side of Tash, whose body was riveting from the sexual ecstasy of being fondled by the two other women. Vicky pulled Tash's body tightly into her own, rubbing her breasts against Tash's to trigger her erogenous pleasure zones. She provocatively slid up and down on Tash. Vicki's clitoris hardening with excitement. Tash was delirious and partly out of it at this stage, although enjoying being the fantasy, "we are going to teach you how Kerrnunous likes to be pleasured so you can pass the initiation tonight. This is how you must give him his pleasure." Tash rolled her eyes back, Nodding and becoming engrossed in their little sexual game.

Returning the kiss to Vicky passionately, who gloated over such a response, they moved Tash sensuously out onto the massage table. The two women lightly drying her sensual oily body as she lay face down on the table. Swapping her wet robe for a dry one. Leaving it gaping at the front, exposing her voluptuous chest and groin. Both women sensually sucking and licking Vicky's breasts, ensuring to sexually please their master, with brutal exciting foreplay, it's the only thing that satisfied her masochistic tendencies.

A gong rang aloud. Warm oils were brought into the room by a tanned young girl who was topless, the lower half covered flimsily with a sheer silk scarf, her nipples tattooed with Kerrnunous symbols, and pierced with sleepers, she poured warm oil on Tash's back and Vicky's naval region. The oil ran down into her groin, spilling onto Tash's butt. As Vicky climbed up onto Tash's body, the three massaged Vicky and Tash sensually. Keeping up the sexual arousal as Vicky continued sensually sliding up and down on Tash's tiny tanned nubile butt, indulging in the pleasure of the fantasy, Vicky loved sex slave games, dominantly ordering them to turn Tash over. Tash was now drowsy and groaning uninhibitedly with sexual pleasure, coming close to climax. Vicky, instinctively knowing this, thrust open Tash's leg to one side. In an animalis tic dominance, impulsively going down on her. Instantly flicking Tash's clit with her tongue, arousing her almost to climax. Then ordering, by the snap of her fingers, one of her sex slaves to pass a vibrator. Vicky moved slightly back and up onto her knees, spreading herself to accept one of the sex slaves, inserting the vibrator inside Vicky so that it would give her even more pleasure. She wanted it in her. At the same time, she sucked Tash's wetness. The others participated by sensuously kissing and sucking them both.

Tash began to orgasm in a frenzied fashion. Vicky came loudly at the same time, then rolled Tash's lower half away so Vicky could selfishly enjoy her orgasm. Amidst it all, a tall person appeared, covered in a white robe with a shroud covering his head, with only the eyes and mouth cut away. The women moved ajar slightly for the powerful presence to enter their sensual circle.

Marion also followed, top half-naked, enjoying the moment, feeling ecstatically aroused, moving to the bottom of the table. Tash still amist of climaxing. The robed one knelt up on top of Tash, also wanting to enjoy the sexual frenzy. Bending to taste her wetness, pushing wide open her legs. The women lifted the robe of Kerrnunous to naval height, revealing a muscular, lean suntanned body, incredibly aroused through having observed the ritual and having to impatiently remain as an aroused watcher. Now it was time to enjoy and sexually participate, suddenly he stuck his hard erect penis into Tash, breaking her hymen. She squealed through the pain in ecstasy. She wanted more. He sensuously thrust into her while the other women stimulated his erogenous zones. He couldn't contain his orgasm in such a tight pussy, that was so wet with desire. It was overwhelming. His body trembled while exploding cum into Tash, impregnating her with large amounts of fertile semen. It had been timed well. She would become pregnant. He let out a large primal masculine cry as he enjoyed the finale of his orgasm, then everybody left the two.

Tash lay delirious, still wanting more. Half-unconscious from her multiple orgasms, as he perversely still used and fondled her body as a tool for his sexual pleasure, knowing they were purely in the confines of complete privacy, savoring the after play for future fantasy.

Twelve

Kirsten, suddenly veering off her course home, opting instantly for a hook turn on the green light, confusing Father Gibson, who clutched the dash on impulse, "this is a bit spontaneous, is it not?", said he. Kirsten agreed but proceeded with determination. "I don't know why I'm doing this, but I'll arrest Daniel just to get him out of there," "canna ya' do that lass?" inquired father. "Well it's probably a technicality, but I'll come up with something that's by the book rest assured," Kirsten replied adamantly. He felt confident, that no doubt she would work out something. Her mind was so astute, she knew the law well and she'd surely come up with the goods.

Pulling up impulsively, the two-hop out of the car. She phoned Paul, notifying him where she was. As he replied, she hung up, being in such a hurry and having no time to loiter in conversation, Father Gibson had already rung the bell. A voice replied to the bell ring and repeated itself. Kirsten assertive demanded, "Open up, it's the Police, Open up now". She shoved her badge in front of the screen, the gate opened and the two walked briskly now to the main entrance. The

Guard alone, standing in the small control camera area. He looked new and nervous. Kirsten instructed him she wanted to see Marion. It was urgent, and he stated that he would page Marion, although as far as he knew Marion already had a gentleman sitting in her office waiting. Kirsten took off toward the stairs, he demanded she wait, refusing to stop she was now climbing the stairs with the Guard in pursuit of Kirsten, who had moved out from behind the small counter leaving the half swing door open, revealing quite a wide expanse of surveillance Screens of the Juvenile Institution. It would appear there were many cameras in all the various areas. Kirsten was moving swiftly up the exceedingly long steep staircase with the Guard in hot pursuit. While that was occurring, Father Gibson, being ever so curious couldn't help moving in closer to observe the large surveillance screens, having a fascination for such amazing digital technology. He had seen this device previously and was quote competent with this IT. He checked from side to side, observing if he was alone in his surroundings, the urge to investigate overrode him. He leaned in, switching and flicking the channels, observing all areas. Two of the cameras were blank, he wondered, why? Fiddling with the buttons, the thud of his loud heartbeat now pulsating, adrenaline rushing through his veins. Praying he didn't get caught, cautious he scanned fleetly for any other nearby safer position. Kirsten would surely kick his butt if he messed up this time. They could go down. This was getting way too dangerous.

The next minute the screen turned on, "Oh my God," he jumped back, scaring himself at the same time getting a slight electrical shock. Low and behold a familiar sight graced the screen, that of what looked like a person from the Kl u K lux Klan. No face eminent, only a tongue protruding through the white cloth licking something, it was hard to distinguish in the lighting, fascination stirred in Father's face, he made the picture smaller, therefore establishing a clearer picture of the surroundings. "Oh, lordy lordy, it's a body. Oh my god," he whispered in surprise, at that moment the hood of the robe moved to reveal the face of Judge Benneton, who began to sexually embark upon the body, completely unaware that anyone was observing him. Father Gibson could hear someone coming, he switched channels, moving away from the counter. Appearing nonchalant, standing to face in the opposite direction, making a speedy effort to appear calm. This was huge, he thought, very complicated. The Guard ran back into the Control Room, paging Marion to respond quickly, who reciprocated instantly to the call.

Father Gibson was worried, where was Kirsten? Standing in Marion's office waiting, a buzzing noise went off similar to that of a pager. Kirsten observed it, picking it up out of curiosity then pressing one of the buttons, the tiny machine turned off. The door flew open, rage projecting from Marion's hardened face, Kirsten hiding the device in her hand. "What exactly can I do for you?" Quickly disguising her anger with an aloof sophisticated facade, to prevent the onslaught of being invaded by the law. "I am here on an inquiry, I must speak with a young adolescent named Daniel, he was witness to an incident regards a past cold case, we need to question him." "Well at present that's impossible, he's gone on a supervised retreat and will not be returning until tomorrow, however, should this need to be done we will also need papers from the authorities, you know, the red tape thing." Marion lightened up, feeling partly relieved as she had controlled that situation well. "Certainly, snapped Kirsten, I will be back tomorrow afternoon. Good day to you." Kirsten slammed the door on her way out. Meeting Father Gibson back at reception, he looked haggard, in silence they hurriedly left the building. As Kirsten drove down the road, he explained what he had seen. Marion now sat in her chair feeling uncomfortable about the situation, she felt suspicious and that this new visit was too easy. She felt that somehow, she had been set up. But how?

Kirsten couldn't come to terms with what he'd described Judge Bennetton, questioning Father Gibson again and again, literally interrogating him. Father Gibson felt exhausted. She dropped him back at the Presbytery, her mind racing in defense, as she'd known Judge Benneton through work and he seemed such a man of integrity. What the hell was going on here?

Kirsten now heading straight for Police Headquarters, moving rapidly through the office, peering into the Sergeant's office. "Got a minute?" she inquired. "For you, anything." She sat down and spilled her guts, not leaving out any detail. Sarge took it all in, "Hmm this is an explosive situation, Kirsten." He stated. "You're telling me, Sarge!" Thinking for a moment, he made a phone call, a Detective would be assigned to follow Judge Benetton, with definite caution. The Sarge would have to contact his more Senior Peers. This was a big shark in a hierarchy position within the Government, that is if he was truly involved, which is yet to be proved. A difficult case that would require specific direct evidence to prove guilt, should he be guilty, but more to the point who else was involved? How many and who? The plot thickened and to what depths in what positions, and to what proportions were the cult controlling internally within the Government and externally? Who could you trust?

Kirsten called out to Paul to come to her desk, "Yeah Kirsten, what can I do for ya?"

"Well Paul, do you think you could tell me what this is?" Holding out the small electronic device. "Looks like it's some type of hi-tech pager or something," he too was curious as to how she had acquired the device, purely accidentally. In her haste to be non-conspicuous Kirsten had stuck it in her jacket pocket, only now realizing she hadn't returned it to its rightful owner. Linda came in to observe the pager

Linda suggested they get one of the guys in IT communications to check it out. Kirsten agreed, explaining quietly to Linda and Paul that some major investigations were to be carried out on Judge Bennetton, his family heritage, etc. Paul was more than obliging ready to assist Kirsten, he'd do anything for her.

Kirsten decided she was calling it quits for the day. She bade farewell to everyone and left the office.

The storm outside arrived in thunderous torrential rain, hitting the roads hard and fierce. It was bitterly cold, and dark. Outside the downpour of rain was immense. Looking up at the ceiling through the skylight momentarily, feeling strangely satisfied. Hidden behind a screen, checking his watch, dressed so professionally in his suit clutching his briefcase, Judge Benneton proceeded to walk down the long wide staircase. On entering the reception area, the Guard paged Marion, who appeared instantly in response from around the corner. Marion shaking Judge Bennetton's hand, in front of two other staff members as she apologized for keeping him waiting for such a long time in her office, and also for leaving him to his own devices when being interrupted to adhere to other work-related issues. "On the contrary," he replied, "it's not an issue, I will however be leaving tomorrow afternoon for Queensland, therefore, I will not be available for three weeks. Perhaps we can re-connect at that point." "Yes," Marion replied, with a nod, "That would be good."

Not speaking a word, she saw him out. As he vacated the premises, he phoned Ramona on the mobile, who as a reliable diligent secretary, had organized his schedule perfectly to suit his every need. Confirming that she would be there in ten minutes to collect him and deliver him home.

As he stood outside the building, the darkened grey skies opened up, spewing forth loud thunderous rain. Lucky he had his umbrella, Melbourne weather was always somewhat unpredictable, he was glad that tomorrow afternoon he would be basking in the sunny tropics of Queensland, it had been such a long-awaited holiday and well overdue. One which would assure him total relaxation and pleasure.

Thirteen

~~~~~

Once again, a dreary Melbourne day had transpired. Zak, John, Daniel, and Tash were ordered into Marion's office. Their bodies motionless, sitting immersed in fear, terrified by what may be coming up next. Knowing the unknown within these walls could often bring death to a soul purely by looking at someone the wrong way, or by saying something out of line. The sad point was, no one would even know you'd disappeared off the face of the earth if you're a homeless juvenile. The Juvenile Institution was so skilled in controlling and engineering every little detail, no one would ever know you were missing or dead.

The teens felt the void of dread. Tash sat on the chair, still delirious from a night of drugs and her secret initiation into her ritual sexual adventure. She looked like something the cat dragged in, still unsure whether last night was a hallucinogenic dream, or her imagination, induced by some type of spell by the satanic witches. Her body flaccid and limp from the physicality of it all. Flung into emotional insecurity instantly when faced by the physical presence of the unaware Daniel, Zak and John seated next to her. The silence was deafening. Somewhere deep inside her, she started to realize that it wasn't a dream. Tash's physical body started awakening to the pain in her body, wondering suddenly if Daniel had observed, or any of them knew what she now thought had transpired the previous night. She felt lost in her teenage shame and half out of her body. She didn't know who she was anymore. Her thoughts intensified, she fought to prevent the overwhelming enormity of it from snapping her mind. Confusion set in overcome by emotional suffocation internally, she had to get out of this warped Juvenile Institution but how? Somehow, she had to.

Marion entered the room, speaking minimally only, asserting her authority, giving distinct basic instructions for their next mission. John stared at her venomously, wanting desperately to tell her where to go. Marion instantly switched on telepathically to his insubordination, glaring directly into him spiralling the intensity of his anger through thought projection, sending his mind and anger back into himself. Anxiety vibrated through John's skinny little body, he felt hatred and blackness penetrating deep within him. It was consuming for such a young fiery soul. He wanted out of the Juvenile Institution as soon as possible. His thoughts rampant with fight and flight however, apathy began to numb him. His legs were turning jelly-like.

The Teenagers were dressed in the green Institutional delegated clothing, then summoned to the reception area after lunch, they were given casual trendy clothing to put on then were escorted out of the building. They sat in the car anticipating the journey, it was the usual stretch to the same old shopping center. Vicky drove, of course she was alone with them today, but who knows how many others were following or who was observing them and how. It was always such a microscopic operation that ran like clockwork. So closely monitored by immense security and Technology. Next minute, BANG. Zak retaliated. "What the hell was that. Get down, someone is shooting at us". They all ducked including Vicky who then accidentally hit the curb hard attempting to steer off the road quickly and safely. The car stalled and rigidly chugged, nearly sending Vicky into the windscreen. The car came to a sudden halt. Luckily it wasn't the Melbourne peak hour. What on earth had happened? Jumping out to check the car for bullet shots, but then realizing the tire had blown and completely ruptured, Vicki approached the rear end of the vehicle to observe the damage. It was very clear that hitting the curb had caused the other tire to become flat as well. Vicki was pissed off. Aggressively returning to the car, grabbing the mobile phone. "I need some assistance," she stated, throwing the phone down, "The battery's flat on this god dam phone. What are happening with these wheels, we have two tires flat?" Silence reigned. Vicki was unnerved and unusually paranoid, compared to her regular hard cold dominated self.

Deciding to lock the kids in and head to the service station to use their telephone. It was the first time no one else from the coven had escorted them, as Marion felt the kids were now so frightened of the power of the coven, they weren't aware that Vicky was their only chaperone and that no one else was around. More paranoid illusions that had been created as a result of Marion's clever mind power games.

As Vicky flicked on the security with the remote control to

lock the teens in the car, in her haste she failed to realize the alarm didn't bleep. Daniel observed Vicky hurriedly heading off to the service station for help. With an accomplished smirk on his face, he turned to the others, he raised his hand throwing into the air the battery from the phone and the car alarm. "Shall we go then guys?" he was excited by the taste of freedom, surprised that the others were all terrified. John's mind racing, "do you think this is a test?" "Maybe, this Juvenile Institution's prone to anything mate, but I'm out of here, ya' coming? At least I got something out of doing the garbage job." Daniel sat hastily thinking, time could not be wasted. Daniel took charge, "We'll split up and meet back where we used to hang out in Reservoir. Zak, you come with me. John you look after Tash, make sure she eats something tonight, use your wits, it's survival mate now go quickly."

Daniel took a deep breath. Zak and Daniel speedily walked into the Mall and disappeared through the Chemist Shop and out the back car park Once on the other side of the car park, they ran for their life. Zak had problems breathing, he puffed and panted and wheezed for intensly, unsure whether it was breathlessness or an overwhelming adrenaline rush from the feeling of freedom, but he was going to run, and run as fast and as far as he could.

Tash, still in another dimension was being pulled headlong along in John's trail. He was focused, he felt his free spirit soar, he had a plan, they were off in the opposite direction to Daniel and Zak. Although he had responsibility, he had Tash and she was dragging her feet. "Get it together Tash," he bossed. She started a peal of hideous laughter, her brain was backtracking and she was still so wasted. She felt like it took a fortnight in time to move quickly through the Mall, her perception of time lost, her mindset in altered slow motion although now becoming aware of her body moving hurriedly. Suddenly John pushed her between the cars in the huge park area, she slumped over clutching her stomach, grabbing onto the car next to her with the other hand, a massive projectile vomit erupted from the pit of her gut, it was all too much for her.

John stopped dead in his tracks. "Shit," he yelled frustrated. "Come on, I know you're sick Tash," he rolled his eyes to the sky he was anxious, his heart pounded, he was on limited time. "Shit," he yelled in desperation. On the spur of the moment he broke into the car he stood in front of. In one swift deer-like action, he opened the car door on the passenger side. For a small skinny chap, fear had bought strength to his body in his effort to escape. He grabbed onto Tash, lifted her into the passenger side, closed the door, he had to get out unnoticed and as inconspicuously as possible.

Tash almost buckled over, dry reaching toward the caer floor. He promised himself he would never commit another crime again, but what could he do, it was do or die. He hoped there was enough petrol to get them to their destination. He thought about driving to the next town. Maybe Ballarat to a refuge to get temporary help for Tash. She was green and he had no medical experience. What the hell was he to do, as long as he was breathing freedom he didn't care, it was only an hour or so down the road, better to go further, what if he went to a hospital in Melbourne and it was part of the cult. They would be up shit creek, then he had to meet Zak and Daniel, they might take quite a few hours on foot to get back to the warehouse, he didn't have time to look for them, he had to act. He felt he had a couple of hours up his sleeve to make sure Tash was seen and got medical attention. It was now his responsibility, he couldn't let Daniel down. Tash looked like she was on death's door.

John drove down all the back streets cautiously not to be noticed, before he knew it, he was home and hosed, out to St Albans. As he neared the corner he forgot to indicate, he wasn't used to driving this type of small car, as he steadily turned the corner heading on the Princess Highway, a loud siren screamed up behind him, he panicked, his biggest fear, "Oh.. no, the cops. Tash get down."

He indicated to pull over. He was going to pull over and jump out and do a runner. As he moved into the left lane the Police car drove off past him in hot pursuit of another vehicle ahead. He quickly pulled over, sighing with huge relief, his nerves were shot and frazzled. "Jesus, that was a close shave," he sat for a moment to collect himself, he couldn't help but think, if he believed in God, he would have thanked him.

Now they were on the main highway. Once again, they were home and hosed, away from all the god-forsaken satanic crap. His little heart sang. What a buzz. After such a harrowing experience he decided he was going to make life work for him and try and become a good person. Crime did not pay, nor does living on the streets, it was only a negative existence in the world of a cesspit. He was going to look after this car and return it somehow to its owner unscathed after his mission was completed.

Fourteen

Daniel had a plan, he would go to Father Gibson with Zak. He knew he would be guaranteed help, safety, and secrecy. They ran through the unknown streets like wild banshees. Daniel became aware of Zak's diminishing energy as they ran in through the school gates. Daniel run directly to the bikes that stood in a line, some of them weren't padlocked. They stole two of the bikes, jumping on in haste pedalling off across the schoolyard madly, the next stop was the service station.

Daniel kept the man at the counter busy while Zak zipped in and effectively managing to steal a Street Directory, shoving it into his large jacket attempting to mask his crime.

Then a distraction occurred purely a fluke and quite unexpected. Zak fainted in complete breathlessness. The man at the counter was compassionately concerned. Daniel and the guy chatted briefly allowing Daniel to regroup. Zak looked shockingly pale. The man suggested Daniel take him to a doctor immediately. "Yes sir, I shall do that now." The two took teens off. With the mission partially complete, Zak's fainting spell and ill health slowed them down considerably.

Taking note of the street and suburb they were in. They withdrew into a new development block of abandoned upmarket units that were being built. Taking refuge for a brief moment to learn their location and get their bearings. Daniel assessing the situation feeling Zak needed a break, he wasn't a fit guy, he was ghostly white and painfully wheezing. Daniel ran out to the phone box out front of the building site He tried ringing Father Gibson. The phone rang four times, then an answering machine spoke, he hung up quickly, in desperation he rang Kirsten's number, she answered, oh my god, what would he say, he hardly knew Kirsten. He didn't know if he could trust her. In consternation, he hung up quickly, after all she was a Cop, what the hell was he thinking.

Running diligently back into collect Zak. It was starting to get dark, Zak was cold, and shivering profusely. "O.K.," said Daniel, "Plan B." He pulled out Father Gibson's business card and checked Kirsten's address on the back. He looked it up in the Street Directory, "OK mate, you ready to go, do you think you can make it to Kirsten's? We haven't got far to go and we'll take the back streets its less lighting and we won't be so conspicuous." Zak replied apathetically, "cool man," he was exhausted, slowly getting up off the cold cement, climbing back onto his small newly acquired dragster bike, a mere pittance of transport, but for now, it served their purpose, they were away knowing it was only around 10 minutes cycle away. Daniel felt Kirsten's place seemed, at this point the best option.

Daniel already had researched the distance from Kirsten's house to the Church. It was close, Daniel felt sure Zak's health would hold up until then, they were only half an hour away from help. They were so close to safety and had to hastily power on regardless in order to make it to their destination. At least they'd make it to Kirsten's. Well they hoped they had the right address. They finally arrived.

They unlocked the side gate and walked the bikes around the back, slotting them in tightly, hiding them behind the small tank stand and fence. The house was in foreboding darkness. As they walked toward the back door the lights on the back of the house switched on. Thank God, thought Daniel, she's home. He knocked loudly on the back door, but alas no one answered. He continued to knock calling out for Kirsten.

The old neighbor came out, speaking loudly over the fence in a friendly fashion, letting them know she'd gone back to work. He then disappeared back into his little abode turning of his back light. They sat down on the back stairs, the lights automatically switched off. They were left peacefully in the still of the darkness. They now had confirmation it was the right house. Next move, thought Daniel, whose mind had not had to be this sharp for ages. Plotting the next move, in the darkness, they could hear suddenly drawing closer by the second, muffled masculine voices emanating from the front side of the house. The two sprung to their feet in flight instigated by fright! They hid in the atrium shrubbery, camouflaged by the large leafy foliage praying the lights would not come on just at that split second. Daniel pulled hard at a wire that was hanging from the light, pulling the whole light down, it fell to the ground although the sound was muffled by the thickness of the plants covering the ground, the broken light rolled away, disappearing into the undergrowth. Daniel could hear himself breathe, he felt like it was echoing in the stillness of the night, although it was not. His breath turned into midst from the cold air as he squatted, making not a skerrick of a sound. In disbelief, they quietly squatted down deeply hidden in the foliage, and from their positions they both observed the two Security Guards from the Juvenile Institution entering. Daniel began to reconsider his position. Suddenly, wondering if Kirsten was involved somehow with this Satanic Cult that dwells within the walls of the Juvenile Institution. Zak quickly covered his mouth in an effort not to cough through fear of giving their hidden presence away. The Security Guards were trying to break into Kirsten's house without being caught, they had some fan dangle super technical machine like a scanner that they ran over the security alarm of the house, but they seemed to have difficulty breaking the code on the house. A car pulled up in the opposite neighbors' drive, startling them. They froze to hide as well, only momentarily, then one pulled out bags of drugs. Daniel and Zak instantly looked at one another, wondering with intensity what sort of shit was going down here now. Whose side was this Cop on? Daniel realized straight away, it was a setup when the Security Guards planted a couple of bags of heroin in the pot plant next to the door, then they took off back around to the front side of the house. Daniel raced over grabbed it, and threw the drugs over the fence of the neighbor. Next minute the dog started barking loudly and went on the attack. Daniel ran back to Zak, he knew Zak would slow him down, so he instructed Zak to stay put. He needed to get to Father Gibson to inform him the Security Guards were after Kirsten and him. Daniel had to let Father Gibson know he was in danger. Daniel squatting quietly, overheard the conversation between the Security Guards. He now knew they were setting Kirsten up.

As Daniel took off around the side of the house one of the Security Guards had come back around the other side of the house to check out why the light had come on. Seeing what had provoked the constant restless barking of the neighbor's dog. The dog becoming agitated and jumping up hitting the fence repetitively on the attack. He signalled to the other Security Guard who had left the back of the van wide open displaying all the junk within.

Daniel made an impulsive decision and one that may never pay off in the long run. He ran opting to jump into the back of their van and hide amongst all the rubbish. He crouched down low, turning off the interior light battery, hiding at the very back of the van amidst a heap of junk and large old canvases, remaining inconspicuous to the human eye. Hidden in the dark using the large black sheets and the rubbish to hide under. Daniel was petrified and couldn't believe what he'd just done, but he had to protect his only hope for the future, somehow it would happen. Daniel hadn't even devised a plan, if he failed, he'd be back at the Juvenile Institution and then he was stuffed. He knew deep inside his heart he could trust Father Gibson, who appeared an honorable man of the cloth. Since re-meeting him again, Daniel had flashbacks regards his early years as a little child with Father Gibson. They were fragmented but he knew they were good moments.

The Security Guards seemed to be gone for quite some time. It seemed abnormally long. Daniel popped his head up impetuously, warily maintaining his invisibility, suddenly he saw them approaching the van, he hid down quickly. The two muscle-bound bounty hunters climbed into the van, the Security Guard driving forward winding down the window halfway. The silence is now deafening. The dog had stopped barking. The next minute, out of nowhere, the angry black dog leap-ed up at the half-open window to take an aggressive chomp at the Security Guard. The Security Guard freaked out with shock, hitting back with force with the baton getting in several blows to the dog's head, and just as quickly winding up the half-opened window to lock out the avenging aggressive attacks by the big black dog. The dog ran around to the back of the van and continued to attack the back door of the van. Daniel's heart racing. The dog suddenly slumped down on the bitumen, severely wounded, panting, bleeding heavily, and struggling for its life. The van careered off swiftly, driving back along the main road toward the Catholic Church. The Security Guard now settled himself and threw his baton carelessly into the back of the van, almost hitting Daniel on the arm. From where it landed, Daniel could vaguely make out the silver part of the baton, which was now covered in a dark fluid. Daniel slyly slipped his finger out from underneath the canvas sheet to touch the baton as the van drove off recklessly. Raising his finger skillfully to his nose, Daniel now realized it was the smell of hot blood. Instantly he knew they had brutally injured the dog in an attempt to ward off the dog's attacks. The cannibalistic bastards had no mercy.

Fearing their psychic radar may detect him, he tried ignorantly to protect himself from being discovered energy-wise. Although he only knew how to pray, in his head, he constantly chanted our father in the hope that it would somehow give him the help to make it through the night alive and set himself free. Allowing him to complete his plight to rescue himself and keep Father Gibson alive. He felt responsible somehow and wanted to find out why he had so many unanswered questions. They slowly drove through the back gates of the deserted, dark, eerie Cemetery. Further along the dirt road quietly halting the van at the front side of the huge bluestone historic Catholic Church. One Security Guard crept stealthily towards the Presbytery building. Through the glass window the building appeared only dimly lit, appearing void of life. The other Security Guard approached the front window of the Catholic Church, spying out from the darkness into the window of the candle-lit historic Catholic Church. The security guard felt the need to enter the premises in pursuit of Father Gibson. Arrogantly approaching the door on his mission to find and dispose of the Priest. Almost robot-like mindset, the Security Guard reached for the huge, large front wooden door, his hand abruptly froze to the large gold brass knob, he stood chillingly set, as if in stone, unable to move, glaciated on the steps. Inches away from him appeared a satanic apparition floating, it was huge, lifelike, and terrifying. Its husky, strong, penetrating voice forebode him to set foot in the Catholic Church. It was against Satan for a follower to do so, the voice forewarned the Security Guard, and he would be tortuously punished as the apparition shot riveting vibrations of pain and horror through the Security Guards' entire being. The Security Guard was then flung by a strong energy force away from the front door of the Catholic Church.

Daniel, now sneaking silently out of the van, undetected

in the darkness. From a short distance Daniel observed in total overwhelming disbelief, the ghastly terryiifying being, he could see it, he could hear it. Was he going mad? Daniel watched the Security Guard flee to the van. Jumping in driving of aggressively to pick up the other Security Guard, as they sped off dangerously into the night.

Daniel ran frightfully around the other outside of the building, panic-stricken the spirit would attack him next. In his panic, he discovered a small, obscure side door. Fearlessly pushing it ajar to slip rapidly through the small door opening, at the same time remaining as quiet as a mouse. Moving promptly when inside. Daniel's eyes scanned the inside of the dimly lit Catholic Church. Immediately he moved toward the confessional box then darting in to hide. On closing the door behind him, the small red occupied light on the outside of his present refuge switched on. Daniel had already locked the door to protect himself. He slumped in the corner in a fetal position, praying repetitively in the quiet furore, he became so drained by the experience. Feeling the exhaustion in the stillness within the confines of his newfound dimly lit hideout. Daniel drifted momentarily off into sleep. He was fighting the drowsiness.

The bright light distracted Daniel instantly, as the small window situated in the middle of the wall loudly slid back, Daniel dived to lean upright against the wall in an effort not to be seen through the caged window. "Hello, blessed be to God, how have you sinned." Daniel jumped up, peered through the window up close, scaring the daylights out of Father Gibson. Daniel attempting to quiet Father Gibson instantly, whispering, "quickly Father, Father they're trying to kill you." Father Gibson, whispering in disbelief, "What would you be talking about lad?" Father Gibson directed, Daniel whispering to cautiously in silence move away from the window. Next minute the wall moved slightly ajar, allowing Daniel a small secret entrance to pass through into the other side of the wall. Quietly Father Gibson crouched Daniel in the corner so he would be unseen by anyone. Daniel knew not to breathe a word while Father Gibson rang his mobile phone, speaking very quietly to his brother the Buddhist Monk. Father Gibson continued for the next half hour, to hear the confessions of some of his devoted followers of the Parish, while Daniel crouched respectfully undetected in the corner out of sight.

The Catholic Church bells rang aloud across the night to announce the ending of confessional service and the closing of the church for the night. Father Gibson drew the drawstring of the small curtain, allowing him vision through the mirror of the inside of the Catholic Church. Daniel marvelled at this secrecy within the Church building walls. Neither of the two uttered a word, ensuring all the people had left the Catholic Church, and the altar boy had locked the front doors and left the premises safely through a hallway. Father Gibson pressed an inconspicuous button hidden mysteriously underneath his seat. Standing back against the wall, the chair quietly and effectively rotated around, revealing a precisionally large circular manhole in the floor, exposing a downward staircase leading down deep into a secret tunnel. They climbed quickly down into it. The movement lights switched on automatically at each step revealing the way ahead in the large tunnel. Above them, the trap door closed over instantaneously.

Daniel felt safe but mystified. He knew nought of such secret passageways in Catholic Church buildings, which made him review his thoughts on the staunch Catholicism upbringing that had been taught to him as a small child. Inside they came to the end of the large stone secret tunnel. Engraved in the wall in large calligraphy writing, the words "Nosa Coso Nostra," embedded in the ancient stone wall. Daniel surprised, turned instantly to Father Gibson's, "That's Mafia," he stated abruptly, "Heavy shit man," said Daniel shaking his head unsure now of his safety. Father Gibson replied, placing his finger in the middle section of the letter and pressed, the word inward lightly which activated another opening in the wall. "Oh hell," stated Daniel bluntly, suddenly flooded by a huge issue of mistrust. Father Gibson aware instinctively of Daniels rising fear, "At a time like this, one must seek sanctuary rather than question its honor," "Daniel we must hurry, time is running out we have no time to argue, you need to be hidden in safety, asap." Running down the thin cold corridor, the sensor lights switching automatically individually off, as they raced along. Entering through another concealed door, once again a Mafia sign, coveting the key which opened the door. This small concubine led up four stone steps with a locked door in front of them, Father Gibson pressed in the code and the doors buzzed open. They stepped through, as they walked out of the double wardrobe doors, directly in front of them stood a small bald man, robed in orange with a happy quiet disposition. Father Gibson bowed to him, and thanked him for coming. Daniel was lost, and a little confused. In his disorientation, he didn't know where he was now, although Daniel realized the building was that of a small specially lined shed. The Monk requested Daniel to sit, he grabbed the razor. Daniel dubiously obeyed Father Gibson, who then explained Bunta was his brother. What they would do was shave his hair, give him an orange robe to wear, and he could stay in hiding with Bunta for the while. No one would know, and it was a great camouflage. The Buddhist Monastery offered a quiet ashram of self-reflection and would be an extremely safe haven for the present. Father Gibson reassured Daniel he would remain in constant communication. Daniel somewhat reluctant, agreed to the Plan. Within minutes they were done, then cleaned up all direct evidence of the makeover. A new transformation of Daniel had taken place. No one would ever be able to identify him, at all. Bunta and Daniel left the small strongly made blue stone-lined shed that looked similar to a bedsitter. He now had his bearings, it was the small building set out in the back blocks of the Cemetery. How extraordinarily phenomenal. Daniel was pledged to the secrecy of this event. As they drove off, Bunta chatted in a friendly fashion, he figured Daniel was quite battered emotionally, so light conversation was only on the agenda. Daniel only half listening now, still worried for Zak, although he felt like he could finally relax a little. Father Gibson tidied up and dissolved all evidence of their make-over meeting. He locked the doors and proceeded back through the dimly lit corridors from whence they had come. Emerging quietly back into the Confessional Box, then out into the angelic atmosphere of the candle-lit Catholic Church, retiring safely to his quarters. Although guarded he immediately contacted Kirsten on his mobile phone.

Fifteen

Kirsten listening intently on the line to Father Gibson, paying acute attention to the resonance in his voice. Paul called from across the other desk, "Phone for you, Kirsten, it's urgent." "Hold it, I'm coming," she spoke into the phone, reassuring Father Gibson, advising him she'd be over later as she had someone else waiting on the other line. She had to go and hung up.

Switching the phone to the other line, it was Steve Jencon, the Plumber ringing from her house. He was distressed. He broke down on hearing her voice come over the line. Linda observed Kirsten's facial expression, which disclosed sudden shock.

"OK, we're onto it, be there in five." She immediately marched into the Sarge's office. Closing the door briefly giving a quick, honest explanation of the shocking news from the phone call. The Sarge decided to go with her. He felt there was danger lurking, and Kirsten needed backup. Linda and Paul also followed as a backup.

They arrived at Kirsten's place. Paul also on guard, checking for a setup. As they came around the back, Steve sat crouched on his knees under the light, very overwrought. Next to him lay the bludgeoned body of Zak. It was a traumatizing homicide visual image. Kirsten instantly consoling Steve and offering support. The Sarge radioed everybody that needed to be notified. The area then became swamped upon immediately by Law Enforcement Officers. It was now declared a crime scene. In hot pursuit, Detectives arrived now wanting to investigate the murderer. Kirsten was definitely in the clear, although it appeared she was being framed. Steve had only come to fix the hot water service. Indeed, he was innocent. Forensics arrived, and several hours after attaining all the evidence for the investigation, they eventually took the body away in a body bag. Kirsten organized for someone to pick up Steve and for him to have a debrief and follow-up counselling. He certainly had never had such a horrendous find when he was out on a plumbing job. When you're a Police person, you can become resilient to this sort of stuff occurring day-to-day. It's just such a regular occurrence, but unfortunately for Kirsten, it was right on her doorstep literally. It was challenging to deal with knowing they may be after her, although she maintained a strong facade. The next minute Shane came rushing through the gate, seeking out Kirsten with intensity. "Are you alright, babe?" He moved toward her to hug her. Her aloof wall went up like a tidal wave. Sensing his physical gesture toward her, she withdrew from his reach. Turning swiftly to enter back into the house to converse with the Sarge and Linda. Paul and Shane glared at each other in dual territorial silence. Shane muttering under his breath, angrily leaving, feeling rejected.

Kirsten rang Father Gibson and requested the Priest meet

her at the morgue. Zak had the tattoo now. Strange, it only looked to be recent. Therefore, Kirsten asked, "Father Gibson bless Zak at least." There was no one else to notify of his death. He was a street kid, after all. By the time Kirsten had arrived, part of the autopsy had already revealed Zak was HIV Positive and his prognosis guarded. The way he was murdered was a lurid immoral way for him to die.

It was going to be a long night and a lot of paperwork. Kirsten would get to that later. Heading straight over to speak with Father Gibson. She said briefly to him as they quietly discussed a plan for some concise resolve at this point. Then she returned fleetly to the Police Station. Typing up Reports for the rest of the night, deciding to have them completed in the early morning. She didn't feel like going home to a macabre execution site at her house. She felt more secure staying back to work at the Police Station. Paul was enjoying the opportunity to keep her company. The phone rang. It was another Police Station reporting to them another murder just out of their immediate jurisdiction. They indicated they didn't have the time or manpower to attend, requesting some help from the Sarge. The Sarge asked Kirsten to join him as it would give him a chance to check in on her. Given the recent ordeal at her home, He felt it better to attend this crime scene to check it out. It was quite a distance out of Melbourne. As they headed off, the Sarge radioed Police Communications, seeking more specific directions as to the location of the crime scene. He knew the area quite well, so they headed off out through the back blocks to Daylesford.

Kirsten wound down the window, breathing in the brisk cold morning air, which gripped her lungs on inhalation. It was such fresh country air, they viewed the stationary Police Cars scattered across the scene along with several unfamiliar coworkers, who had partitioned off the area with red and white tape. They drove in, parked the Police Patrol Car, then walked toward the crime scene activity area of the isolated expansive car parking bay situated slightly away from the main highway. One side of them looking downfield from the huge clifftop was a sheer drop many meters downward leading into a large chalet of open bushland, a rather Brobdingnagian Australian scenic view for tourists. Hanging precariously on the cliff face a small car dangerously balanced, making the investigation quite unsafe and time-consuming. Kirsten stood with the Sarge horror-struck looking inside the vehicle at a very young lifeless skinny body, stabbed numerous times in the chest, a colossal dagger ruthlessly wedged into the tiny body pinning it to the driver's seat. A prominent symbol was painted in blood on the windscreen of the car. It was that ill-fated tattoo sign again.

As Kirsten approached, she identified the body instantly. It was John, what a direful murder. Half mutilated, he was painted all over with that same symbol in blood, which was sadistically macabre and an alarming sight to behold. Kirsten almost vomited, and as she stepped away slightly, the scene had left a sour, bitter taste in her mouth. Sarge got the details relaying them immediately to Kirsten, who stood motionless, staring at the horrendous scene before her. She moved even further away discretely. According to Daniel, she rang Father Gibson, who informed her, Tash was with John when he'd last saw them. Kirsten quietly came back to the scene, checking the passenger seat for clues. Drawing this information to the attention of the Forensic Investigator on hand, who then found a couple of long blonde strands of hair, but they had to be identified, of course. Kirsten was shattered. She wanted to go home.

On returning to the Police Station, Paul suggested Kirsten grab some casual clothes from home and crash at his place for a day or so, just to be safe. Paul was always prepared for the perfect opportunity to present itself. Kirsten, torn, then agreed. She was so exhausted, she just wanted to sleep. She was emotionally shattered with no fuel left in the tank. Linda came into the office at that moment, "I'm always here if you need anything." Kirsten, grateful for her offer, opted to go with Paul. Before leaving the Police Station, Forensics rang, concluding there were also blood DNA stains from another source. The other Police were now combing the rural area, looking for a murderer or someone else who may have been murdered or involved in this sorrowful homicide in the rural outskirts where the parking bay was located.

Kirsten crashed out on Paul's divan then awoke after ten hours of a dead sleep. She took a shower, got dressed, ate a small meal that Paul had prepared, then politely and gratefully left to discretely meet with Father Gibson in his Church Chambers.

Father Gibson divulged all information Daniel had disclosed, leaving no detail except where Daniel was hidden. Although Kirsten felt it was better, it remains a secret for the moment, given the ordeals of the previous night. Kirsten was glad to know how Zak had gotten her address. Father Gibson explained even her sharp, perceptive eye had missed that bit at the time. Daniel was quick and clever, and at the point they were at, it was too coincidental that the body was found at her house. No doubt it would be sorted out and the investigation prove a great deal. Father Gibson definitely, at this stage, needed to remain anonymous, and his meddling in Police business continues to be unknown, especially to the Catholic Church and to the Sarge.

Kirsten ran a check with the Detectives. Discovering that Judge Benneton was still out of town. Returning to the Police Station, only to be greeted by Linda, "Mate, I've been trying to ring you on ya' mobile. Where have you been?" "Shane's been looking all over for you." "Hmm," sighed Kirsten with her cool-like style, not that perturbed. "Linda, I'll get changed into my uniform. I need your assistance." Kirsten looking a little vulnerable. "Sure, what'll it be? I'll finish this Affidavit, and I'll be with you." Quipped Linda responding. Kirsten advising, "We're doing a house call," By Linda's facial expression, she appeared very interested, "OK, who on, Shane?" Kirsten impatiently responding, "No, not him. I'll explain shortly." "OK" Kirsten retired to the locker room to change into her uniform.

As the two pulled out to drive off, Father Gibson saw the Patrol Car leaving. He desperately needed to divulge some further information to Kirsten. Father Gibson quickly followed them. Hoping to catch up to them at the lights and hail Kirsten down. But that didn't happen, and he found himself continuing to follow in hot pursuit. By the time he did catch up, they had already parked the Patrol Car and entered into the Junoesque mansion front yard, and disappeared swiftly around the back of the building. Father Gibson sat for a moment in his car, anticipating their visit would only be a brief one. Father Gibson whistled some Irish tune and fidgeted impatiently with a piece of paper. The next minute a car drove slowly up. Observing the Patrol Car, he recognized it from the Institution. "My god, what gives," he whispered. It stopped momentarily and drove off.

The two women had not come out. Worried Irrationally, he rushed from his car around to the back of the house, catching Kirsten and Linda in the midst of breaking in through the back door. "Would you two be committin' some crime then?" he said, relieved with a laugh. "Oh no," said Kirsten, "not you. What's up now?" Kirsten is exasperated. Father Gibson laughed and whispered to them about the car out the front that had just checked out the Police Patrol Car. They felt an urgency to check inside the house, tidying up any signs of their investigation, so no one would notice and hoping to leave with some type of direct evidence to incriminate Judge Benneton, something worthwhile to have him in for questioning.

Once they were inside, they found the large house to be filled with darkness. They quietly scanned the place, ready and on guard with weapons blazing. This was real Police stuff, thought Father Gibson, who swallowed hard and decided he was going in too. He entered the stately lounge room. They checked out the rest of the house, finding no one and no direct evidence of any substance to their plight. Father Gibson waited for the two women to appear in the lounge room. He listened to the message on the Judge's tracker pager and held up the photo from the ornate over the mantle. Whispering, "look at this, Ladies, did you see this?"

Linda grabbed the framed photo silently, then handing

it to Kirsten, "Shit, he's a twin!" They covered up any signs of being there in the house, and all promptly left. Linda, in a bullying tone, warned Father Gibson not to speak a word. Otherwise, she'd charge him with hindering the Police and breaking and entering. He chuckled to himself, leaving so as not to cause Kirsten any unnecessary strife. The two women radioed to communications, seeking more information regarding Judge Bennetton's never before heard of a twin brother.

They returned to the Police station to draw a description photo of Judge Benneton and seek information about his brother's name and particulars and any other details that may be relevant to their investigation. Doing an intense background check to also see if the brother had ever committed any crimes or had any driving offenses from which they could seek an address.

The two women both had to attend an armed robbery, so they left it in the hands of Paul. Good ole' reliable Paul.' He was pretty happy to play the desky tonight and stay in the Police Station, just to research a case, rather than race around out on the road playing cops and robbers. The two women headed out in a hurry and returned just as quickly.

On their return, Kirsten dropped Linda outside the Police Station. She was just going down to the shop to get some Chinese food for everybody's dinner. Kirsten was about to get out of the Police Car as the mobile rang. It was Father Gibson, who quickly informed her that Judge Benneton had just returned home. Kirsten drove straight over to the house. As Kirsten was approaching, unnoticed by Judge Benneton, who'd driven off already. Kirsten discovering Father Gibson's car parked hidden out of sight. Kirsten pulled up behind Father Gibson's car. Immediately she jumped in his vehicle and ordered him to drive. They followed straightaway unnoticed and remained undetected. As Judge Bennetton neared the Juvenile Institution, it was growing dark. Kirsten rang the Police Station and informed Sarge of her plan. The Police swiftly got organized to catch up to Kirsten and started their strategic plan of attack regards Judge Benneton. The lambent sizeable full moon rose amid the stormy dark cloud-covered sky. Kirsten constantly updated the Sarge of their whereabouts as they headed out toward the Christmas Hills behind a fleet of slow-moving cars. It was a long procession with a foreboding unknown destination.

Father Gibson broke into a nervous sweat, but he felt compelled to open his heart, "You're a wonderful young woman, you know, my dear. I feel we're close to solving this ya' know, and I just wanted to let you know I pray every night for you and that you're protected by the angels, so ya' know they'll always be lookin' after ya.'" "Thanks, Father," Kirsten replying with a tone of endearment. She looked at him with a warm fuzzy feeling in her heart. Kirsten did have a fondness for this very challenging man, who was a funny character. They'd kinda' bonded, despite the constant ordeals and his mischievous infuriating nature over the last few weeks.

The picturesque full moon shone through the windscreen, creating an eerie visual atmosphere. The cold mist seeped throughout the trees, causing a low ground misty fog. Kirsten and Father Gibson drove quite a distance back from the fleet of cars ahead to not be too conspicuous but still cautiously able to pursue their prey. A sudden cold chill whisked through

Kirsten's body. Intuitively she knew something was coming up. "Stop for a minute," still maintaining contact on her radio with the Sarge. "How far are you guys?" she inquired, "We're almost organized and on our way," he replied. "This is going to be a big job. We're going to pull over and park the car in the bush and walk. It seems like they've slowed right down and entered some sizeable open clearing." "Sarge, hurry and get here, I've got a strange feeling about this, and we're a long way off the main road." "OK. I'm on my way, Kirsten. You can handle it. You'll think of something you always do."

By the time that Kirsten and Father Gibson had secretly waded their way through the bush unseen. The people already had a scene set with some strange type of stage erected, unusual neon psychedelic lighting powered and ran from a generator, creating a bizarre illuminations effect out in the middle of a forest. There was a crowd of about a hundred feral hip pie-looking crazed people gathered. Kirsten wondered if that was how they dressed all the time or were costumed for effect as part of some weird film scene. The atmosphere was negatively energized and dangerous. There were constant loud drumbeats and a chilling shrill chanting, ear piercing to Father Gibson, who was unsure if they were added sound effects emanating from the big Woofer speakers. He knew now for sure, as all signs indicated, it was definitely a Satanic Coven Event. He breathed deep and expected the worst. He knew how Satanic Witches could be. Barbarically debauched compared to White Magic Eclectic Healers. He knew they were going into a dangerous heavy unknown situation. He blessed himself, quietly asking God for protection under the light of the full-blown lucent moon.

They observed vast amounts of LSD, speed, and other hallucinogenic drugs being given out to the masses. In a few minutes, most of the feral s were out of it, speaking in tongues and garble, singing, chanting, and screaming with weird laughter, adorning a giant statue of Kerrnunous with their semi-naked bodies dancing around carrying out wildly bizarre sexual antics.

This was bizarre behaviour to Kirsten, who now expected the worst. It made her question how these people live. This to her was indeed an unusual reality. The atmosphere began to heighten as if with expected anticipation. Then, a pompous figure entered the stage, completely covered in a black robe from head to toe. The masculine voice spoke assertively and dominantly to everyone in the crowd, who looked on in awe. He announced the marriage of Vicky to Kerrnunous. She emerged onto the stage in a see-through black flowing gown, supposedly a satanic wedding dress, fully into her huge sexual ego. So proud, feeling like royalty, and thought she was above many others. Her arrogance strongly imminent in her swagger on the stage. To the primal deafening drumbeats.

Drugs were constantly being handed out. Kirsten knew she had at least reasonable cause to arrest them all on drug charges, so that was something to work with. She had direct evidence. Kirsten and Father Gibson were crouched down, hidden well out of sight in the thick foliage, still observing the bizarre antics of all. Kirsten's mind ticking over constantly with her strategic plan. "Father Gibson," she whispered, "try and get on the other side and keep down. Take this gun." She always carried a small gun strapped to her calf, just in case she needed that extra protection, Father Gibson questioning her motive, "What would I be needin' a gun, for now, missy?" "Take it," she bossed. "Alright, alright, I wouldn't even know how to fire the thing, lass." She turned to him and said, "Just act, make out if you have to."

Surprised, he responded, "OK, OK." He took off toward the designated area Kirsten had delegated. It was a very dark, deserted area. Father Gibson had tried to get through the pine trees that were laden thick. He had to break some branches down to create a pathway to enter through. He seemed to have to go further away from the scene to get over to the other side. Father Gibson regarded his location. It was so dark, with no light provided for him to see clearly in these surroundings. He was disorientated by the darkness. Danger lurked, but he could not let Kirsten down. Tripping on the rocks, rapidly falling to the ground, unable to breathe a word to expel his sudden pain, badly injuring his knee, he awkwardly got up in agony to continue his mission, having no time to mess about. Finally, in a sweat, he reached the other side, collecting himself and trying to get over his temporary physical disability. Meanwhile, the Ceremony taking place was becoming hideously bizarre on stage.

"What a croc," scoffed Kirsten, whispering to herself. Still observing the riot, checking to view the outskirt boundaries of the scene, trying to decipher if Father Gibson made it to the other side. Father Gibson, on the other hand, finally had made it to a more prominent safety spot. Here there was a little more light in the vicinity for him to see where he was hiding. Father Gibson could at least see now where he was stepping. Suddenly feeling strange, he had been walking on very hard, what he surmised to be branches, but the light of

the opulent moon revealed them to be that of human bones. He felt sick in the guts instantly. Instantly reaching for his abdomen. Father Gibson was aware he couldn't move beyond this position as he would blow his cover.

Having to be stationary at this point and maintain obscurity was a priority. Now he had a full view of the scene ahead. Six men carried onto the stage a large four-poster bed and placed it toward the back of the stage, to the side of the altar, next to the large wooden cross positioned upside down. On the large back black screen, the Coven's large symbolic tattoo was placed as an artistic visual piece of artwork flapping gently in the breeze. Some loud, daunting exorcism music penetrated the air, mixed with the roaring primal drums. It was all part of the ritual, obviously adding intensity and effect to the Ceremony. Incense burned and wafted through the forest air, conjuring up the demons.

Father Gibson prayed. He knew that he was a likely target, being a Catholic Priest and knowing the evil power of a Satanic Cult and the depth of its psychic ability. Aware of his fears regarding this scene, Kirsten and he were playing with fire, but it was too late. They were already immersed within its perimeter. The surrounding atmosphere changed to dark and creepy. Father Gibson became aware of a being emerging on the stage. Goosebumps ran along his arms, making the hairs stand on end. His heart thudded in the dark as his stare fixed in full vision of the stage. As if out of thin air, an extraordinarily handsome, magnanimous man appeared. Father Gibson wondered if anyone else could see him. Some paid homage to such a vision of a man. Some were too far off their face on drugs to comprehend its existence.

Father Gibson thinking for a split second. It could be trickery by some camera technique, such as he had already observed over the weeks with all this futuristic high-tech equipment that the cult owned. Reassuring himself that it was real. When the magnanimous man's hand raised itself to move Vicky's blonde hair from her face to kiss her cheek, she glowed as any radiant bride would, looking at such beautiful physical perfection in the form of humanness. The High Priest united them and ordered them to move to the four-poster bed to consummate their marriage.

The see-thru curtains were let down around the bed, and they stepped up onto the bed as though everyone else had been shut out and disappeared. Vicky was captivated by the romance of her partner as she lay down on the bed amidst the crowd's noise of hysteria. As she closed her eyes in fantasy to take him in sexually, she felt sudden incredible pain, like a knife had slit her insides. It shocked her as her eyes flew open. In fear, suddenly, the beautiful man had turned into Kerrnunous, a demonic-like being with horns and an ugly lizard-like body. In an instant nightmare, her temporary illusion was shattered. Caught up only in a monster now. She suddenly felt violated and reverberated by the physical shock of the grotesque urchin on her. She screamed, and it beat her aggressively across the head, almost knocking her unconscious. It was brutally attacking her sexually.

Vicky was in immense physical pain, almost blacking out as her womb was being perforated. As she screamed, no one could hear over the hysteria of the crowd. As the being ejaculated, it spoke demonic filth to her. When it had finished using her body for its sexual pleasure. He threw her out of the curtained bed, back onto the stage near where the High Priest stood holding a chalice to the sky.

Marion appeared, dressed in some weird witches' gown, and swaggered ruthlessly, bearing no heart to the battered crippled victim Vicky, lying in total pain in a catatonic position on the stage. A gold chalice in her hand, she raised it to the heavens and to the full moon's glory. Marion was known as a mere maid, the elite High Priestess of the Cult.

Vicky begged for compassion and help. Coldly, Marion cruelly glared at her pain, parted Vicky's legs slightly, and pushed with incredible force down on Vicky's lower abdomen. She screamed in anguished pain, her body becoming listless from shock. The action caused Vicky's vagina to let forth a massive hemorrhage from the womb. Marion grotesquely collecting its blood into the chalice. When she collected some of the blood, seeking adoration from the crowd, she raised the chalice again, leaving Vicky squirming around on the ground, fearfully clutching onto life, lying in a bath of blood, and now semi-conscious. The crowd in heretical chanting

Next encore, Tash was dragged onto the stage, everyone screaming in an excited frenzy and clapping manically. She was naked, her nipples pierced, her breasts branded with the tattoos of the Coven's symbol, a dog collar around her throat, her labia even ringed, with loops and chains attached, a masochistic sight to behold. Tash was utterly drugged. Her soul fragmented entirely to the winds, with welts all over her body from being whipped. Kirsten had never seen this in a real-life situation. She was dumbfounded but still watched on impatiently, awaiting the arrival of her colleagues. She prayed they hurry. Afraid of what was next. She was stuck and couldn't do much on her own. She had no backup. Frantic in her mind now, "Stuff this," she said under her breath. She had to do something. Someone had to stop these psychos.

The High Priest stood on the stage with a satisfied look of great power as Tash's blood trickled down his chin. Holding the dagger in one swift movement, he slit Tash's throat. Father Gibson prayed, immobilized in trauma, observing such an act from such a barbaric human soul. In a dark hour of total need, he knelt, praying for Tash's soul to be redeemed. His warm heart deep with compassion, suddenly unable to breathe. He grabbed his throat. Someone had placed a rope around it, creating a vice. He fought for his breath as three huge Security Guards beat him and continued to strangulate him. They doused his body in some strange fluid-like substance, drenching all his clothing, they dragged him kicking and fighting toward the stage. Kirsten viewed this interruption from a distance and became angst.

The Security Guards threw Father Gibson up onto the stage, then three Security Guards hung him upside down on an upside-down crucifix. That was it. Kirsten was going in. Marion enjoyed the pleasure of ripping off some of his clothes and turning to him in her cold, aloof tone. "What a pity, what a waste of such a good athletic body," she snubbed as the High Priest glided toward him with a candle, "perhaps Kerrnunous will enjoy this offering as well." Aggressively, he threw the candle at Father Gibson, who instantly caught on fire, the flames almost blowing him up. The solution he was doused in was highly flammable. He screamed and screamed, trying to put the fire out. His screams were bloodcurdling. Kirsten ran in, guns blazing, care less about the danger she raced in to save

Father Gibson. A dozen Police Sirens sounded throughout the immediate area. Police dogs barked loudly and pounded in to attack. The Coven was busted. It was on for young and old. All of the Star Force suddenly present and forced to act. A helicopter flew over top, beaming down giant rays of light igniting the area.

Kirsten raced to Father Gibson amidst the chaos. Her only mission to save her friend from burning. She threw her jacket on his burning flesh in a primitive effort to put out the flames and help him. The Police quickly swooped in and arrested most of the people. Ambulances were called to take care of Vicky and Father Gibson. Kirsten couldn't touch him. He was so severely burnt. She consoled him gently as he lay on the stage in agonizing burning pain. A true unsung hero. A tear slipped down the side of Kirsten's face, exuding a sad loss, given her fondness for the man. She felt she hadn't told him enough what a good soul he was. Kirsten could not express her thoughts as she crouched close to him in sadness and quiet disposition, emanating only a pure love from her heart for him. With a weak hand, Father Gibson reached up. He was still there, not entirely gone, "Kirsten, I'm still here, pray with me, child." Relieved slightly but feeling his pain, she tried desperately to console him. Linda looked on in silence, moving next to Kirsten placing a compassionate hand on Kirsten's shoulder.

The Ambo's arrived instantly and attended to him. Kirsten rode in the Ambulance with him, constantly adhering to his wishes. They arrived in Emergency at the Hospital. Kirsten was relieved to see her dear friend Gail was on duty, a Charge Nurse, so proficient at her job, Kirsten knew he was really in good hands. Gail took over and allowed Kirsten to remain. They chatted briefly while Gail worked to relieve some of Father Gibson's physical pain as much as she could. She looked over to Kirsten, "How are you doing?" she inquired with empathy. "I think it'll be another long night," Kirsten replied, "Yes, do you need a coffee?" "Yeah, you go get one and come back when you're ready," replied Gail. "Thanks," Kirsten replied in appreciation. "Gail, do you think we could call his brother, I don't know of any other immediate family members, but I know his brother's phone number. He's a Buddhist Monk." Gail replied, looking down at the badly burnt body on the bar-ouch, "Yes, I'll do that. It's extremely appropriate at this point."

Kirsten went to the machine for coffee, returning hurriedly in case Father Gibson had passed away. She wanted to sit this vigil out, as she could see so sadly, there wasn't much hope for him. Returning after washing her face to stay awake, she sat with her coffee staring at him. He was hallucinating, so the staff said. Kirsten felt like he was talking to angels. She could feel something around her. Some supernatural presence but a positive protective one. Bunta arrived with another Monk from the Buddhist Monastery. People stared at them as they were quickly escorted by Gail, down to Intensive Care and into the private side. Father Gibson was in a remote section now. Bunta, on entering, was speechless, his eyes filled with tears for his dearly beloved brother. He'd bought his beggar's bowl and filled it with water.

Pulling out a reel of special gold thread, he gently tied it to Father Gibson's finger without causing any unnecessary pain. Father was heavily sedated by morphine at this point and now quite delirious. Bunta expressed his brotherly words of devotion before death struck. It suddenly dawned on Kirsten that the other Monk present was Daniel, who was now aware she'd just realized it was he. According to her intense stare. He smiled at her and nodded reposeful. She spoke to him quietly. "the obvious is often the most overlooked." softly marveling at Father Gibson's ingenious idea to hide Daniel as a Monk. No one would ever realize nor worry too much about investigating the matter further to find that out, especially as Daniel was a homeless person of no fixed address.

Bunta graciously handed Kirsten a book. She thought it read the Dharma treasures, inquisitively she inquired if Bunta could briefly explain what they were doing. He said she was most welcome to participate. They would join the thread between each other, make a triangle, and chant healing tones. It was part of their ritual to help dissipate pain in someone's body when humans were sick. She participated in a second, having no clue about the Buddhist words she was chanting, only hoping it would help to ease her dear friends' horrendous pain.

They chanted for an hour, continuously making sure they had privacy, and they weren't disturbing anybody else. Father Gibson seemed to become quieter, more relaxed considering his present state of being, and peacefully gently slipped into sleep. He took his last breath and passed away into the afterlife. Kirsten felt left in a void. Bunta stood then left the room, bringing his brother's death to Gail's attention.

Kirsten still sat as nursing staff came in to organize the body and turn off the IV Medivac. Bunta asked if Kirsten would like to go with them or be dropped off at home. "What will you do now?" she said to Bunta. "Return to the Monastery and pay homage to his reincarnation. Assisting his spirit in passing over," "Does that take long?" Kirsten inquired. "No," he replied gently, "half an hour or so maybe," "Can I come?" quipped Kirsten. "You're most welcome," he bowed, "Our Guru would be most happy." They arrived at the Buddhist Monastery, taking off their shoes outside the front doors in respect, placing them on the shelf, before entering into a sizeable gold-clad room filled with monstrous gold statues of Quan Yin and Buddha. It oozed wealth and prosperity. The energy revitalizing and so peaceful. Chimes played gently in the wind as Bunta quickly prepared herbs to be burned for this ritual. They sat crossed-legged on the floor before the prominent relics. Kirsten didn't care that she had become involved in another religion that may breach the laws of Catholicism. After all, it wasn't harming anybody. It was for a good cause. It was paying her last respects to her dear friend Father Gibson. Bunta placed a wooden cross in front of them to show respect for their dead brothers' religion. He then focused on Meditation conjuring in the spirit of his dead brother. Father Gibson appeared in spirit in white light as if out of the abyss. Daniel looked on in awe. Kirsten could see what she thought was a ghost. Bunta chanted, reaching out to touch the white light apparition. Father Gibson bade Bunta and Daniel farewell. Father Gibson turned to the apparition of Ester, who also appeared and who held out her hand to accompany him into the light. Father Gibson's ghost then looked to Kirsten and said two words, "Thank you." Kirsten felt the presence of his energy, feeling overwhelmed by the mystical ghost-like experience. She waved, too afraid to move in case he disappeared. He smiled, and Bunta delivered a verbal chanting Buddhist blessing. Daniel was mesmerized. Tears slowly slid down his face. The Buddhist gong rang emanating throughout the peaceful walls of the Monastery, and the angelic figure dissipated back into the white light of the afterlife, leaving three large bay leaves in the waft of a slight breeze. Bunta collected them in silence,

He crushed them in a little wooden bowl, walked out into the open door of the magnanimous beautiful atrium garden, and threw them to the wind to set Father Gibson's spirit free. Bunta returned to speak, "one physical finality is sadness, but only for ourselves, as we miss the presence of that soul, but his soul is free to evolve in the conscious realms of a new journey. We must acknowledge this and not grieve for too long but celebrate his legacy of his souls' journey."

Kirsten was stunned by such a new and unusual concept of death. It always seemed so final to her. How interesting, though, at least this way she knew Father Gibson's spirit hadn't entirely gone from her life. He would always be floating around her. She could indeed cope with that, which meant that she could still talk to him even in spirit. Anything's possible, she reassured herself.

Sixteen

As Kirsten left the Buddhist Monastery, she felt better, even though experiencing such a harrowing ordeal and deep sadness by the sudden loss of Father Gibson. Bunta dropped her back at the Police Station.

Kirsten arrived back inside the Police Station. Paul rushed attentively to her side to make sure she was OK. The Sarge came out to check on her as well. "Kirsten, that was a job well done. The two High Priests got away, though, amidst the bust." Kirsten stopped in her tracks. She was so disappointed to hear that news, given Father Gibson's treacherous death. She thought the case would all be over, finished, and closed. Now sadly, it didn't seem to be so. Shane appeared in a burst of verbal rage, ordering Paul to get his arm off of Kirsten. Paul stood fixed, although his arm tightened around Kirsten's arm in a territorial effort to protect her. Kirsten moved forward, and in one swift movement, King hit Shane, who landed with a thud on the ground, momentarily losing consciousness. Shane Shaking his head while trying to pick himself up off the floor. Kirsten looked directly in the eye at the Sarge, "in a court of law that was provoked." Shane then yelled. "You can't do that." Kirsten, as smooth as silk, replied in her calm manner, "I just did."

The boys in the office congregated to view the drama. Abruptly she stated, "I'm tired. I've had enough. It's time for me to go home." She vacated the room. No one spoke, but their Victorious smiles were for Kirsten, not for Shane. The Sarge turned, "Well, boys, it's back to work then. There's a lot of paperwork to do."

Paul watched Kirsten get into her car and wearily drive off home. He stared at her in admiration, thinking, 'what a woman.' Shane broke out in a sweat, then severe heavy chest pain set in. He was in bad shape. The Sarge realized there was something majorly wrong. He made the call to the ambulance. The Sarge helped administer first aid but was lost as to what was wrong with Shane. The Ambo's whisked Shane away quickly, notifying the Sarge later that Shane's pituitary gland had had a minor bleed. Although he was going to be OK, Sarge was unsure whether to let Kirsten know or not. He'd opted to tell her later and discuss this further with her once she had had some sleep. The Sarge knew she needed a rest, she was a strong woman, but the woman deserved a break. She'd been working non-stop on this case for weeks. He'd tell her once she'd had a chance to sleep. Maybe Kirsten would be in a better frame of mind then.

The next day bought with it a hive of activity to get the case solved. There had been enough bloodshed. On arriving at work, the Sarge did explain to Kirsten that Shane had been carted off to the hospital and asked if they could discuss this later as Shane was quite unwell. Kirsten, momentarily worried, shifts her focus, and then they got down to business.

They would set up a raid on the Juvenile Institution, making use also of Star Force for a robust backup, who knows what else they'd be up against, especially after last night's strange caper had given so much more insight into how sadistically the Cult operates at times.

Ready and on fire within a flash, they headed to the Juvenile Institution. Once inside, Kirsten exerted her authority, "Where's Marion?" she implied. The nervous Security Guard replied, "She's on holiday." Kirsten runs up the steps of the staircase, then bursting in aggressively. Gun in hand and loaded only to find Marion's office vacant ultimately of her presence. All was deathly still. She opened a door while no one was looking. She dropped in the tracker she'd accidentally taken on her recent visit, quickly observing that it was on. She didn't have time to switch it off as the security cameras watched her, but she was somehow smart enough for them to miss her action. She left the office instantly, like an agile hunter on a rapid mission. Kirsten was gonna' get those bastards for killing Father Gibson if it was the last thing she'd do.

The Police dismantled after finding not a skerrick of evidence in the Juvenile Institution or any clues as to Marion or Judge Bennetton. Kirsten felt defeated by their investigation quest, but she was determined she was settling this case today. Kirsten returned to Police Headquarters. Marion appeared out from the secret panel of the wall, sitting now in her office to deliberate her next move. She had to leave this position and disappear as an individual without a trace. Marion was on the run but to where. She opens the secret door and heard a minor hit on the wall, realizing it was her tracker, at last, she had found it. Lucky it never went off when Kirsten was in the room, she thought. Marion's cover could have been blown. He picked up her emergency packed small suitcase, gathering things out of her top draw then climbed down the grand staircase for the last time. She looked back for a fleeting moment to reminisce. Hoping in her fast sports car would offer protection from the prying eyes of the public, with its tinted windows.

Leaving the premises, she drove down through a secret underground tunnel that came out in a back street, utterly undetected by any Police Officer or Detectives. Knowing only too well, the Police were surveying with vigilance. The tracker on the passenger seat started bleeping, picking it up quickly to grasp the contents of its message. It was Judge Benneton. She hit the brakes. Where was that bastard she hadn't heard from him? The message read, to meet him at his house. No one knew from the Police Department it was her car. It was registered under a different name. Therefore Marion could disguise herself as a man and go to the house. That's what she'd do in a flash. She pulled over in the park, went to the toilet block, changed clothing, and came out dressed as a man. There appeared to be no one around. Judge Benneton had parked miles back and entered his house through a secret entrance, hoping no one had observed from the Police Department. The house was being watched. Even at a time like this, a man of his audacity had his fears. What on earth was he coming back here for? He had to get a few things of importance anyway.

On entering, he sat patiently on the couch awaiting Marion, who arrived up through the trap door on the floor as well. "You bastard, you took off and left me there." She was livid and continued venting at him. "More like the other way around," he snapped back narcissistically, the intensity of anger inciting the lust between them. "How gutsy bringing me here," said Marion. "No, you called me here," They bantered. She started stripping off his clothes. "How manly of you in this suit," Judge Bennoton smirked, "let me help you out of it." "How apt," sarcastically replied Judge Benneton as they passionately moved toward the bedroom, stopping to the side of the hallway at the lounge. He physically bent her over the back of the couch and aggressively penetrated her from behind with strength. Both their trackers went off in the background, bleeping into oblivion? As the erotic hard passion evolved between them, they moved together further into the bedroom. He threw Marion on the bed and rolled her onto her stomach moving swiftly back on top of her. Judge Bennetton, climaxing, ejaculated into Marion's anus. He came with an incredible roar of pleasure.

A distinctive 'Click' sounded throughout the bedroom. Suddenly bringing him back into reality, he felt something at the back of his head. "One false move, and you're stuffed," stated Kirsten in a strong, clear voice. He froze mid-motion. Shocked, Marion fell flat on the bed face down. The three Police with guns raised held them hostage. Judge Benneton moved slowly by dominant direction of Paul off the side of the bed. Kirsten was about to instruct Marion to get up when Judge Benneton subtly leaned over to the side of the bed and made a quick grab for a small gun under the bed. He aimed it directly at Kirsten to shoot. Kirsten yelled, "Drop your weapon' Linda suddenly appeared out of nowhere and shot now at Judge Bennetton straight in the heart. He dropped dead instantly. No one flinched. Kirsten fixated kept the gun hold on Marion, who, like a leopard, rose on all-fours facing the wall and very slowly turning slightly to move to one side of the bed, standing still for a brief second then turned around to face their hands in the air. Kirsten and the Sarge stood in masked horror. Marion was fully physically nude and exposed to all. She was a hermaphrodite. What a unique vision for Kirsten, who had never seen two different gender forms in one body. Kirsten remained cool, holding it together although masking the fact that she was stunned. Marion, uncomfortable with her exposure, grabbed the sheet to cover herself in desperation, grabbing another small gun that lay next to the bed. Marion swiftly aimed at Kirsten. This time the Sarge yelled, "drop your weapon!" Marion did not adhere, and he raised the gun instantly at Marion. The Sarge shot Marion in one direct hit, straight through the head, causing instant death. The bodies lay slumped over each other coldly on the bedroom floor. Blood awash everywhere in the bedroom. Still, gun raised and in shooting position, Linda took a deep breath, her hands trembling slightly. Police ran throughout the house, checking the rest of the house for any other Offenders or further danger. Paul's phone rang. It was Tommy. He explained the twin brother was an escapee and pedophile of high intellectual prowess that had been admitted to a psych ward in an Institution with schizophrenia way back. On one of his relapses, he had brutally murdered some woman who'd professed to be a witch, so the report reads, stated Tommy. "How come you couldn't find it before," asked Paul. "It's been wiped off the computer, and the records had gone missing. We found them hidden in Judge Benetton's locked office drawer." "Oh, good work, my man," said Paul, "catch you later." Paul then instantly informing the Sarge of the update.

As they sat, taking a moment out to collaborate on the shooting event and debrief. One of the other Constables at the premises who was downstairs called out to the Sarge, "You better come down to the cellar and take a look at this." The three went down the stairs, which lead to a cellar. There, frozen in a large cylinder tube, was a body. It was the real Judge Benneton. The naked body is packed implicitly in ice and well preserved. His throat cut, which had caused his death. "How much murder must one take in a day," sighed Kirsten. Nervous anxiety made her feel sick.

They moved back into the lounge to clear up more details and collect more evidence than the four of them debriefed. Kirsten picked up the trackers with a smile on her face, "Good things these little devices, even if I must say so myself." Admiring her idea quietly to herself, it had paid off to set up the tracker with these paged messages. Linda coming back into the room agreed whole-heartedly. Linda shared filtered water with her comrades.

The other Police were left to clear up the mess, Linda stayed back with them. Kirsten, Paul, and the Sarge headed back to Police Headquarters to tie up the paperwork, writing up the report on such a macabre alarming case. Kirsten decided to take some time off in lieu, heading off home for the day, opting halfway to go over to the Buddhist Monastery to let Bunta know Daniel was now well and truly safe.

She rang the bell of the Buddhist Monastery, overwhelmed

suddenly by the feeling of peace. Satisfaction in the mind that it was now all over, relief overcame her. Daniel appeared. A vision of peaceful serenity. He bowed. Kirsten filled him in on the details briefly. He turned again to honor her. "Thank you, Kirsten, for showing me the road to my enlightenment, for the awakening of my soul. I was lost. I am grateful and happy and will be forever grateful to Father Gibson for the generosity of his heart. It's so interesting that I now know so much more about him and the connection to Ester." He bowed to her. Kirsten smiled and bowed back, compassion in her eyes. "Thank you, Daniel. See, it's not what life deals you with. It's how you deal with it." She smiled sweetly, "I must head on home now. I need some rest."

Her mobile rang on walking down the stairs leaving the Buddhist Monastery. It was Linda again. "Kirsten, Shane's in hospital still. He's in pretty bad shape. Shane's calling for you. Your friend Gail rang from the Emergency Department to let you know he wants to see you. What shall I tell her?" a silent beep, then Kirsten answers, "Tell her I'm on my way there."…….

And we leave them there.

The End… for the moment.

About the author

Karen Power has a unique and fresh approach to storytelling. Her writing draws on the essence of her life experiences and inherent natural affinity with the metaphysical.

She has worked as a nurse, screenplay writer, background extra, and has written several novels and screenplays. Karen is the producer, writer and director of a short film titled "Raphael", showcasing on Prime Video Amazon, which has won several International Awards.

Karen is the author of *The Lighthouse,* a supernatural romance thriller; *The Golden Phoenix,* a supernatural crime romance thriller; and *KAJO,* an Australian adventure romance. Her work is available in paperback, e-book and audiobook formats from your favourite bookstores. You can order online, or enquire with your local bookshop or library.

For more information about Karen's current and future works, please visit: **www.karenpowerfilms.com.au**

Thank you for supporting an Australian writer of original, creative content. If you have enjoyed this book, please consider writing an online review.

Milton Keynes UK
Ingram Content Group UK Ltd.
UKHW021037021124
450589UK00013B/913

9 781763 575301